Pipe's Dream

Road Warrior's MC
Book Three: Pipes & Trinity

BY:

Raven Featherwood

In Appreciation

Writing these books, and living with these characters in my mind has been an adventure - for me. But for my family, well, maybe not so much. I want to thank my partner and best friend, **Danny Bell** for his love and support while I journey into my fantasy world. Thank you for loving me and putting up with me. You are my inspiration babe. I am blessed to have seven amazing children who have given me thirteen (so far) wonderful grandchildren who light up my life. Now, I get to claim Danny's four children and his beautiful granddaughter too, so my cup does runneth over.

If you are fortunate enough to find friends who will encourage you and to advise you, and well, to just be there when you need a shoulder, you know what it means to be blessed. I have many that lend me strength, give me a shoulder to cry on or an ear to bend when I need it. I would need a book to list you all, but daily I am encouraged by **Thomas Long**, a true wordsmith, **Betsy Perez,** more than a sister, and **Penny Matthews**, what did I do without you? My Beta Readers and fellow writers who will read, critique, and be lovingly honest are a critical part of the process and I have had several exceptional ones.

You are all appreciated. **Janet Bingham, Kasey Hill**, and all my friends on the RWMC Facebook page, thank you for coming into my life and loving the Road Warriors as much as I do.

I want to give a special shout out to **Enticing Journey Book Promotions.** Ena and Amanda are amazing women to work with and in addition to promoting this book created the beautiful cover and teasers.

Raven

Prologue

Pipes: (nineteen years old)

Getting my full patch into the Road Warriors is fucking amazing! At nineteen years old I am already a full patch member, a dream come true. Both my brothers were patched in today too, Riley and Rayne, my twin brothers are as excited as I am since they have wanted to be members of the Club for years. We recently started a new band, we are calling it Pipe Dreams. Ranger is letting us play for the bar here at Mother's a few nights a month to get our sound out. I am the lead singer and since Ranger's wife Josie likes my voice she always tells me that I have a mean set of pipes, so my road name is Pipes. Most people that hear it think it has something to do with the pipes on my bike, which I must say are amazing, but no, my name is based on my vocal pipes – rather than the metallic ones. My brother Riley has a road name too, it's Styx since he plays the drums, another Josie naming. Rayne doesn't have a road or band name, but I started calling him Fiddle since he plays the violin, but no one is daring to call him that since he said he'd kill anyone who did, and Rayne is kind of mean sometimes, so he is getting his way on this one.

Tonight, is a big patch party, three new members to the Road Warrior family. The party will start as a family party and the kids will be here for a while, for the barbeque and some of the music, then the real party starts! Man am I happy. I've never had to look for women, not since I was sixteen with a full beard and being so tall with my athletic body and long golden hair. Women

1

love me, hell I lost my fucking virginity to a teacher in eighth grade and have been getting steady pussy ever since. She taught me some serious skills! To say I love the women would be like saying the night has stars. I fucking LOVE women. All kinds of women; black, white, brown, yellow, tall, short, big tits, little tits. I just love them all. No two women are alike. Each woman I take is different and unique. With so much variety I have a hard time understanding how any man can settle for just one. Makes no sense to me.

I'll admit, the club whores and sweet butts do bring a lot to the desire to join the MC. But, primarily I joined to have a family of sorts. Sure, I have my brothers, and my sister Caroline. But, our parents died years ago. My brothers Rayne and Riley are the oldest and were eighteen when our parents died, they had to step in and take Caroline and me from foster care. I was only a year behind them, but Caro was four years behind and only fourteen when the folks died. Rayne took actual custody of us. That was two years ago. She is sixteen now and still a child, but Rayne treats her like she is a baby, not a teenager. I needed more than my brothers and sister, I wanted Josie, my friend's mom, to be my mom. I wanted to spend the holidays with the Flanagan's and have family time where Josie and Ranger would treat me like I was their family too. I needed some kind of parental connection. My mom had been wonderful, but she was always under the thumb of our father, a brute of a man that used her and beat her. But, unlike my home life as a child, Fox and Penny have an amazing family life. Josie always makes me feel special, and Caro loves her and Penny. It just made sense when Fox and Joker decided to prospect that I prospect too. Then my brothers decided that if I was going into the MC, so would they. Ranger himself sponsored all three of us in. God, what a feeling of acceptance.

Pipe's Dream

I'm a Road Warrior. Tonight, we party, tomorrow I'm getting inked by Sinner! Fuck, I am happy, and with all the club whores coming to the party, and all the sweet butts in the playhouse, I'm getting laid anytime I want, and now for the family time. Just what I wanted. A big family barbecue, complete with parents, kids, and even little ones playing in the grass. Ranger and T-Man made steaks, hot dogs, burgers, and ribs! What a spread. All the old ladies brought food too and Josie made my favorite cake, pineapple upside down. I'm going to start with dessert.

Walking over to the table where the sweets are I go up to the cake to cut a piece when one of the most beautiful girls I have ever seen comes up to scold me for having dessert before I eat.

"Hey there, you need to eat first! It's bad for you to start with dessert."

"Yeah, I know, but I like Josie's pineapple upside-down cake, I'm afraid if I don't get a piece now it will be gone by the time I get around to getting a piece of it," I tell her, smiling into those pretty brown eyes.

"Yeah, Aunt Josie makes killer cakes."

"Who are you?" I ask her.

"Trinity, Joker's sister, T-Man is my dad," she tells me.

"Why haven't I seen you around before?"

"Dad keeps me on a tight leash. Still in high school, and my part-time job is at Pin Stripes, so I don't have much free time.".

"The bowling alley?"

3

"Yeah, dad runs it so I work as a waitress or ticket taker, whatever he needs."

"Would you like to go out sometime? Bowling maybe?" I ask with a laugh.

"Sure, but you have to ask my dad or Ranger. I'm kind of off-limits."

"Ok, I'll ask. Just want to bowl, not seduce you."

"Good thing, friends is good, anything else and you'll eat a fist."

"Well, babe, you are drop-dead beautiful, but there are a lot of women that won't get me beat down. Let's be friends," I tell her.

"Sounds good. I bowl every Tuesday at nine." She says.

"It's a date," I tell her. Then I watch as the lovely creature takes my plate of cake, picks up a fork, and turns with a wink and walks away, cake and all.

Chapter One

Pipes (four years later):

Another Saturday night at Rage, I love the band scene. It is so much fun! I knew that having a band would be amazing, but it exceeds all my expectations. In just four short years we've cut an album and made a local name for ourselves.

My brothers, Styx and Rayne still play with the band, our sister Caro plays keyboard when we are comfortable with the venue, and we have a brother from the MC that plays in our band also; Winter is one of the most popular men in the band with his jet black hair and deep black eyes. He is hot and scary all at once.

One thing for sure, the women love the band, I never have to go without on nights we play. I have a hard time sometimes picking which babe to grace with my big badass cock. One thing is for sure, I have never met a pussy I didn't love, and everyone is different, variety IS the spice of life. I haven't had a single one that would make me give up the variety that comes from the multitude.

In the back of my mind, I think of Trinity and her beautiful body, made for love. She is sex personified. Everything a man like me could want to make me rethink my lifestyle. But, she is off-limits and only available for quiet lonely dreams, I have to keep my mind off her. She isn't for me, or any frother for that matter. That has been made perfectly clear by her dad and Uncle.

Tonight, she is here, in the crowd. I am always aware of her when she comes into a room. She draws me, it's like my spirit knows when she is near. Can't explain it, it just is. Ever since I met her all those years ago, she is never too far from my mind. I

5

tell myself over and over that she isn't for me, we are just friends. Too bad I can't make my body accept it.

Tonight, she is dancing with a man that is way too old for her and only after one thing. I'd like to kill him for even touching her while dancing. Not my girl, not my business. I need to distract myself from her presence. A group of chicks are ogling the band and I see Rayne going over to meet up with them, I join him. A cute blonde with big tits sees me and wraps herself around me, found my piece for tonight, she'll do.

I glance back over the woman's head to see if Trinity is still with that same man, but she'd moved on to another, younger man. More her age, but FUCK, I can't take this shit.

We used to be good friends. We bowled together, swam together, hell I taught her to ride and went with her to get her first motorcycle. But then I took her to her Senior Prom and we started making out. It nearly got out of hand and I had to stop it. After that every time we'd get around each other we couldn't deny our mutual attraction. We just stopped hanging out together.

Joker was curious, we'd been good friends, now we didn't even talk. I just blamed it on age difference and the fact that I'd rather be eating pussy than babysitting. He accepted it, what a fucking lie. Yeah, I love women, and I'll fuck them all. But not once has a single one made me forget those first innocent kisses and touches of Trinity.

Trinity:

What the fuck is wrong with me? Why do I feel this way over a man that obviously isn't interested in me? I mean I thought we'd felt something for each other. We'd been so close, then that fucking prom and those amazing kisses and touches. I know he felt something for me. I was so sure I'd end my virginity that night, with Pipes. But no, I guess my inexperienced kisses were not enough for him. He turned me down flat, took me home two hours before my curfew, and left me. Probably to go fuck some club whore who knew what she was doing.

Now, it's hard to even go to Rage to dance without seeing all the women fawn all over him, and he gives any of them what they want – but not me.

Trinity (A few weeks later: Clubhouse Party):

I felt so hot tonight! So many men to dance with! And Pipes is nowhere to be seen so I don't have to have my style cramped by seeing him with his lap full of club whores. Rory and Cat and I danced tonight. It is great to see Cat doing so much better. Fox doesn't let her out of his sight yet. But that is ok, as long as she is improving, that is all I care about. I love that girl.

I've had a few drinks and with my attire being a bit too biker bitch for my folks, I think I'm going head to out. I parked my bike in the clubhouse lot though, so I have to head that way to get out of here. I'll look for Rory and Snake before I go so I can say goodbye to Rory. Snake's new woman is good for him, she's still a bit scared of the MC and all we stand for, but I hope I can become closer to her and she can accept us. Snake will never leave his family, and he loves her, so she needs to learn to love us.

I grab a bottle of water from the kitchen then head to the clubhouse. I see my brother in the hallway, arm around the waist of Candy, one of the sweet butts, seems I am not the only one calling it a night.

7

"Night bro, I'm heading home," I tell him.

"You ok to ride girl?"

"Yeah, only had a couple of beers, I'm drinking water now. Besides, I live all of four miles from here. I'll be home soon enough."

"K brat, get going then. See you tomorrow, Sunday Supper kiddo, this weekend is at mom and dad's," he reminds me.

"See you then." I head into the clubhouse, I start to look around, hoping to see Snake or Rory so I can tell them goodbye. The party is starting to heat up in there though. A woman is sitting on a man's lap, grinding like she is about to get off. What a slut, I'd never let a man get away with that. He needs to work at getting me off, I'm not just riding his fucking leg or crotch for my release. God, woman, have some self-respect.

Another woman has a man I don't recognize over in the corner, he is standing, leaning into the wall and she is kneeling and sucking him off. Others are doing other things that indicate they are going to hook up.

I'm still looking for Rory when I see Pipes. He is across the room. He has a very scantily dressed woman with him. Her breasts are about to fall out of her tiny top and he has his arm around her and his hand on one of those round globes. Her legs are parted with his knee between her legs and she is smiling up at him in invitation. I know I gasp, but god it hurts. I turn towards the door and start to run, I have to get out of here. My own clubhouse has become too hard to be at. I need to stay the fuck away from this MC.

Pipe's Dream

Christy sees how upset I am and she follows me out of the clubhouse. I just run to my bike, but I am crying now and she won't let me get on my bike. I just sit on the pavement and cry. Snake eventually comes up and picks me up, rocking me until I settle. Eventually, I get my shit together and I pull away from everyone that wants to comfort me. They all will be making love tonight with someone, while I lay home alone and cry myself to sleep. I don't want their comfort. I just want the fuck out of here.

Pipes:

I stayed out of Mother's tonight so I wouldn't have to see her dancing with other men. She is over twenty-one now. And even though I hear the women talk about her still being virginal, I also hear them talking about her plans to get rid of said virginity. It is something that I can't think about, the man that will have her for her first time. It won't be me, so I have to make myself not think about it.

I have this cute blond bitch with big tits hanging on me and I figure, what the hell, she can be my pussy de jour. I'm feeling her up and getting friendly when I hear a gasp and look up just in time to see Trinity turn and run from the clubhouse. I see Christy give me a nasty look before following her out. Fuck, I hate hurting her, but I can't have her. I need to move on and so does she. Snake looks around and then follows her out. Good, she has her friends. She'll be ok. I am about to take the woman into the playhouse to forget, even if it's only for a while when I hear my brother Rayne talking to Rory.

"Snake went to talk to Trinity, she saw something that upset her," Rory says.

9

"Pipes knows Trinity has had a thing for him for years. He needs to move that shit to the playhouse when he knows she is here. Damn it, he knows how she feels."

I see Snake return, alone, and hear them ask him how she is, his answer breaks my heart.

"How is Trinity?" Rory asks him.

"Not good, she was sitting on the fucking pavement sobbing when I went out there."

"Fuck" Rayne says, shooting daggers at me from his eyes.

"Yeah, she finally settled enough, she left on her bike. I would have taken her home but she said she wanted to be alone, try to ride it off."

"I'll call her in a bit, make sure she got home ok," Rayne says.

"Thanks, I was going to, but if you are, I'm going to take Rory upstairs." Snake says.

"I got her brother, I'll be sure she's ok," Rayne says.

I can't handle anymore, I grab the woman and take her to the playhouse, where I use her body to do my best to forget my broken Trinity. The woman I'm destined to care the most for, and never have.

Chapter Two

Trinity:

My besties are finally getting their lives together. Soon I'll get mine together. Cat's doing so much better. She and Fox are starting to really look happy again. And I never thought Snake and Rory would ever get their shit together, but he finally got her to forgive him and accept being his old lady, tat and all! I am so happy for him. I never thought he'd fall in love again or trust love again after losing his first wife to a shooting.

Rory still needs to get comfortable with her role in the MC. There is a party tonight, her first as an old lady. So, I took my friend shopping and we are dressing her for success! Her last experience, when Snake blew her off for a club whore was not good for her self-esteem, so tonight she is going to blow his mind, along with all the other men.

"Are you feeling it yet Rory?" I ask her.

"Wow, Trinity are you sure this is ok? I feel kind of naked," Rory says.

"Girl, you've seen those bitches at the clubhouse, you need to show them you can not only win your man but keep him. And, you need to own that cock girl, he's yours, and that's final."

"Girls come on, we are late!" I hear Snake call out to the closed door.

"In a minute, be patient," I shout back.

"We'll be right out babe," Rory calls out to him.

"Well come on then." He isn't hiding the impatience in his voice. We only make him wait another moment before I walk out first. Let me say, I am all sex and hot biker bitch. Snake pales and begs me to tell him his old lady isn't dressed like me.

"Trinity, tell me you didn't turn Rory into you?" he asks me, I just laugh.

"Fuck me," he says.

Then Rory comes out, and I see him taking her in from hair to toes. Her hair is in a sexy half updo. Her make-up is striking and the clothes she is wearing, well damn, she looks hot if I do say so myself. I had her wear a dark red strapless top that molds her body and is braless. Her nipples stand out and are puckered. I see him take a gulping breath as he looks at her. Hot damn, score! Her pants are tight, leather, with black lace instead of material in some very special places, with cut knees and slits up the inside and outside thighs. Black heels make up the rest of the outfit and she has a black leather studded belt twined three times around her waist, the buckle hanging enticingly over her mound. But what really makes his eyes go all hot is the black leather choker that she has around her neck, it matches the belt and is hot as fuck.

"Rory, can we stay home doll?" He chokes out. I look at Rory and she looks at me and we both bust out laughing. Not happening buddy, she is going to run you ragged tonight.

Before long we are pulling into the lot at Mother's. After the last episode, I plan to steer clear of the clubhouse, so I park in the front lot of Mother's. Snake goes around back by the clubhouse, he is planning to stay overnight so I get that. I don't plan to and I want to party!

12

Pipe's Dream

The lot is full of brothers, and other partygoers as I pull into the lot. I'm no fool, I look fucking hot tonight! We have brothers from the San Diego club here as well, something is going on between the two clubs so there is a fairly large contingent of the brothers from that charter here, which was all the reason we needed for a party!

When I get off my bike and pull off my helmet I know all eyes are on me. I shake out my long blonde hair and I know I have the interest of every man in the lot. I'm not supposed to ride in heels but fuck it, I did, and I am strutting my stuff as I head into the bar. Most of the guys know me, know my dad and uncle so they don't hit on me, but I get wolf whistles even from them.

I stop off at the bar where Grizzly, the newest prospect gives me a once over. I just smile and ask him for a beer. I drink half of it down quick, then set it on the bar as I see Joker heading my way.

"What are you wearing Trinity?" He growls at me.

"More clothes than most of the bitches here, brother dear."

"They are whores, you are not."

"Nope, but I'm going to have some fun and see if I can find someone to spend my night with, so back off brother, I want to dance, and as handsome as you are Joker, you are not who I want to dance with," I say, then march into the crowd, dancing by myself until a man whose rocker arm says California on it comes up and takes my hand.

13

He is handsome, in a rugged way. A big man, with a shaggy beard and blue eyes, he'll do. Not as beautiful as Pipes, nor as handsome as Snake, but fuck, a girl has to dance!

"Hi there handsome, what's your name?" I ask.

"Flash," he says.

"Ok Flash, I'm Trinity and I want to dance all night long."

"Let's dance then babe."

We are dancing, grinding, and I am forgetting everything but having some fun. I'm young and tired of holding out for the man I told myself I'd give my virginity to when he doesn't want it.

We dance like that for a couple of songs when Gunner cuts in. Now I like Gunner, but he's Vegas Club, so he won't touch me, even to dance with. His dancing is so distant and barely touching.

"Gunner, why did you ask me to dance. You obviously don't want to touch me, so why?"

"Joker asked me to get you away from that San Diego brother. Trinity, they don't know you are off-limits girl, you are playing with fire."

"Don't I fucking wish" I say, then "Listen, I'm a twenty-one-year-old fucking virgin thanks to Joker and Uncle Ranger, and of course my dad. I am tired of this off-limits shit. I want to have fun and by gads, I will find someone or I'll fucking leave and go down to Rage and find someone!" With that, I turn around and walk back to the bar getting a second beer.

14

Pipe's Dream

That is when I notice Pipes is sitting at the bar, hitting the shots. I decide enough. So I walk up and stand right next to him.

"Pipes, what the fuck is wrong with me?" I am done wondering.

"What do you mean Trinity? Nothing is wrong with you."

"Dance with me then," I challenge him.

"He looks at me, really looks at me. Then he fucking shakes his head.

"You and I both know it isn't a good idea for me to touch you, why do you push it?"

"Why is it a bad idea? You don't care about me, I'm not even good enough to be a friend anymore, not since that night at prom. I heard you told Joker that you don't want to babysit anymore. Is that all our friendship was? Babysitting?" I don't even wait for an answer, I just turn and head out the side door to the lot. But this time he follows me out and reaches out and grabs my arm, pulling me around to face him.

"Trinity, it isn't that you are not good enough, you are too good for me, and your dad will never let me date you, let alone claim you. You fucking know that! You are just torturing us both with this sexy poor me attitude. You need to move the fuck on, I'm trying to move on but I can't when all I see is that sad face when we are around each other."

I'm stunned, did he just say I'm being pitiful, well in so many words anyway. I'll fucking show him pitiful.

15

"Look, Pipes, you and I both know there is something different with us. Our attraction isn't a crush, it isn't normal. And as much as I hate it it's not fleeting. I've tried to date, tried to fuck, but no one is you. You, Mr. man whore don't have the same issue. But, I will find a man who makes me tingle in all the right ways, and I'll fuck him, and I'll move the fuck on. Bet on it! I am not so pitiful that I will fawn after you forever. I just hope that when you wake up and realize all the club whores and groupies in the world won't touch your soul as I would have, it isn't too late."

Then I kiss him, passionately, and fuck yeah he responds. He grabs me, pulls me into him, molds our bodies together, grabbing my hair in one hand, and pulls my head back to get a better angle on the kiss as his tongue invades my mouth, pulling a deep moan from my throat. His body responds to mine and it is like the world fades away. There is nothing but the two of us, melding into one.

He grabs my ass and pulling me tight into him I feel that magnificent cock of his, hard against me. I start to grind into him, then I remember, he doesn't want to claim me. He told me to move on. This is only for pity. Fuck that! I pull back, I look deep into his lusty eyes, and then I tell him what I think.

"Tell me you feel that strongly just kissing your groupies, that feeling, that chemistry we have, it isn't normal and I've been trying to find it for years with anyone else, I can't. But go on, find them, fuck them, I don't need your pity. I know I care for you, but I also know I will go on without you. I may never find that same connection Pipes, but I won't wait for you forever. I'll find someone to love me. Just remember how good it could have been between us. Now, I'm off to Rage, where most of the men don't know I'm fucking off-limits."

Pipe's Dream

I leave him standing there, looking after me as I get on my bike, without even putting on my helmet, and heels and all, I ride off into the night. I don't go to Rage. After that earth-shattering kiss, I could no more touch another man than I could fly to the moon. That kiss wrecked me. Fuck, will I ever get over that man?

Chapter Three

Trinity:

These last months have been tough. Rory's dad hid her in a safe room until she had to be hospitalized, it was bad. I think Snake would have killed him if it wasn't for the fact that he was Rory's dad and she obviously loved him, even if she was mad as hell at him.

There is a birthday party tonight for her, Josie went all out with the food. Her dad is supposed to come, Jen, her stepmother is at the clubhouse already. Some weird shit is going on with that mess, but not my issues. I'm just looking forward to seeing everyone tonight. I've been steering clear of the clubhouse. Too much emotional bullshit trying to deal with the Pipes issue. I think I'm ok, I think I can see him without making a fool of myself.

Even if it hurts, I am determined NOT to let anyone see it. I even have a date for tonight. A nice computer science major from UNLV. He's hot looking, rides a Harley Sportster, and has money. We've been dating for a few weeks and so far so good. No real hot and heavy chemistry, but he is good for my ego. This is the first time I've invited him to a club family event. He knows a bit about the club, so I think it will be fine. We won't stay too late.

Gregg and I arrive just when the food has been set out on the tables. We get in line, grab a plate of food, and find a seat. I introduce Gregg to anyone we run into as my boyfriend. He is a body-builder so his muscles rival the guys here at the MC, and he is dressed in tight sexy jeans, biker boots with silver buckles, a Kings of Leon tee with a black leather vest, and aviator shades. He looks hot. He could rival any of the men here except his vest is just black leather, no patches.

Pipe's Dream

I dressed the part tonight also. I want to make an impression when we are dancing. I don't care what mom and dad think. I have on skin-tight almost see-through pants, hot as fuck with built-in panties. I know that the pants don't leave much to the imagination and I am hoping that I get to stamp the V-card tonight. I certainly dressed for it. Even if Gregg doesn't rock my world, he is handsome, and his kisses don't leave me cold. My top, which is a halter with fringe, doesn't hide my new piercings. It's thin enough that even with my lacy bra the rings in my nipples are noticeable if you look. I am wearing six-inch fuck me heels and I'm still shorter than Gregg.

"Trinity, hey girl, who is your sexy friend," Rory asks as she comes up to us.

"Rory, this is Gregg, and Gregg this is our birthday girl, Rory." I get the intro's out of the way.

"Hey there, you know Trinity long?" she asks.

"A few weeks. We've been dating pretty much every night for the past couple weeks."

"Well good, glad you are having a good time. You dancing tonight Trin?" Rory asks me.

"Oh yeah, wouldn't miss a chance to dance. Live band tonight or DJ?" I ask her.

"Pipe Dreams," she tells me with a knowing look.

I shrug, he told me to move on so, I'm moving on. "Great, they play wonderful music. Gregg you like Indie Rock right? Pipe

19

Dreams is a band made up of MC club members, they are a cover band, playing a lot of Indie Rock," I explain.

"Yeah love it," he says.

"Good, should be fun," I say. Then we get up to walk our paper plates to the trash and as we go around the corner to head into the bar, we come face to face with Rayne and Pipes.

"Hey, Trinity! How are you doing babe? You haven't been around much lately, where you been girl." Rayne asks me, obviously trying to make conversation.

Pipes just looks at me, taking in my clothes and getting a pissed off look on his face, then he looks to Gregg who has his arm around my waist.

"Hey Rayne, Pipes. I hear you guys are playing tonight. I want some Kings of Leon, ok?" I ask.

"Sure babe, who's your friend?" Rayne asks. Pipes still hasn't said a word.

"Guys, this is Gregg. Gregg two of the band members and good friends of mine; Pipes is the lead singer, and Rayne is his brother and plays one mean-ass violin."

"Hi, nice to meet you both." Gregg holds out his hand. Rayne takes it and shakes it, Pipes just looks at him and doesn't take his hand.

"Trinity," Pipes says. "Your dad and mom are in Mother's, you'd best avoid your dad unless you have some actual clothes to put on," he scowls at me.

Pipe's Dream

"Pipes, I am twenty-two in two weeks. I don't care if my dad and mom like my clothes. As I've told you before, I have on more clothes than most of the bitches in the Clubhouse. Get the fuck over it."

Then I grab Gregg's hand. "Come on Gregg, let's go get a drink and I'll introduce you to my parents. I'm sure my brother is around somewhere also. I'd like you to meet him. He's your biggest opposition to overcome."

"Let's do it, baby, I need to clear our path with the parents and brother if we are going to pursue this thing," he smiles down at me. Then rubbing my hair out of my face, he tucks a strand behind my ear as he nods goodbye to Pipes and Rayne while pulling me against himself and leading me away.

As we are leaving I hear Rayne laughing and Pipes calling him a fucker. It's nice to be on this side of the coin for a change. Poor Gregg, all his touchy-feely stuff doesn't affect me like a mere look from Pipes.

As we are walking into the clubhouse, Gregg stops me to ask what is my relationship to Pipes.

"Did you date him?" he asks me.

"Yeah, for a minute in high school. He took me to prom, kissed me, and then dropped me like a hot potato." I tell him.

"Damn, what a fool. Looks like he still has feelings for you though," he is looking intently into my eyes.

21

"Tough, he had his chance," I tell him, then I pull him into the clubhouse.

Pipes was right, dad and mom hated my outfit, but other than a disapproving look, they were so happy to see me dating, anyone not in the MC, that they let it go and welcomed Gregg. Joker on the other hand didn't behave as nicely.

"Trinity Flanagan, where the fuck are your pants!" he shouts at me when he comes up to Gregg and I are standing by the bar ordering a drink.

"Gregg, meet my big brother, Joker. Joker this is Gregg, my date," I tell him.

"Hi Gregg, Trinity, the pants! Where are they?" He is incredulous.

"Joker, get over it, mom and dad didn't have the coronary you are having."

"Yeah, and they go home early. I have to keep an eye on you, not fair brat, go change clothes. I'm sure you have some jeans in your room upstairs."

"Fuck off Joker," I turn and ignore him. Gregg is laughing down at me. I warned him about Joker.

"Big brother is protective I see," he laughs.

"Yep, but I let him, then I do whatever I want. Sometimes I know I cramp his style. When he has to keep an eye on me he can't take off to the playhouse with his club whores."

"Is that a big part of the MC?" he asks.

"Yep, you'll see. In another hour there will be more nearly naked women here than most men see in a year. A lot of them will go into the playhouse with the brothers, a lot of them after the families leave will also go into the clubhouse. Random sex all over the place."

"Damn, maybe I should join," he laughs.
"Nice, here with me and you are into club whores? Good way to find yourself without a date."

"Trinity, there is no woman here as stunning as you are babe. You have no competition," he tells me with a glint in his eyes.

We find a seat where we visit with King, Fox, Cat, Snake, and Rory until the band starts to play. Then Rayne shouts out that the first song is a request from one of his favorite girls. Then they start to play Kings of Leon, *Sex on Fire* and I jump up laughing and pull Gregg to his feet. I shout out a thank you to Rayne and we go front and center and start to dance. This song is one of my favorite songs from the Kings of Leon and I am dancing to it with Gregg and we are laughing and touching and it is amazing to not feel pitiful in his eyes.

I feel him watching me. I don't care. I'll be gone before they finish so I won't have to watch him with other women. But, I'll leave him with a vision of me with another man.

Several songs later, and much grinding and touching, I know the set is nearing the end. I look up into Gregg's face and leaning up into him I ask if he'd like to get out of here.

23

He smiles down at me and kissing me softly, he pulls me tight into his body, right there in the front of the stage. Then, pulling me off the dance floor he leads me to the door, where he parked his bike, then putting me on the back of it, he climbs on and we leave. I am hoping he is taking me to his apartment. But instead, we end up at my little apartment. He gets off the bike and leads me to my door. I am excited, I'm going to do this! But he stops me at the door.

"Trinity. I like you, a lot babe, I would take you in there and fuck your brains out, but I don't enjoy being used."

"What?" I ask although I know.

"Pipes, you still have unfinished business with him. I felt his stare all night, and you were more passionate with me tonight then you have ever been. If I thought that passion was for me, I'd bury myself so deep in you that you'd never forget me. But it isn't for me, it's for him," he tells me.

"No, he doesn't want me, he told me to move on, so I am," I tell him.

"He wants you, I don't know why he is resisting but he wants you, and Trinity, you want him. I don't want to be a fill-in fuck. Go get your man babe, I'm just sorry it isn't me."

Then he turns and walks away, without a backward glance. Damn.

Pipes:

She is here. After all these weeks, she is back. But she isn't alone. She has a man with her. Not a boy, a fucking man.

Pipe's Dream

And he knows I want her. He looked me right in the eyes and put his arm around her pulling her into him. Fuck.

One look at her and my cock went rock hard. Jerking to attention and reaching towards her. I didn't try to hide it, but she didn't look at me, she looked at him. He is walking with her, away from me in those nearly see-through pants and halter top from hell. And fucking A her nipples are pierced! When the fuck did she do that and who the fuck did it? Who had their hands on her nipples? FUCK! This is too much. And I have to sing tonight and watch her dance with him. How?

"Damn Pipes, you fucked up brother, that is one fine woman. You should have fought for her. Now he has his hands all over that fine ass." Rayne is pushing my buttons.

"You know they would never have let me have her, no matter how much I wanted her."

"Well, you'll never know you pussy, you didn't even try" and now he is walking away, shaking his head.

He's fucking right, I should have tried. But I didn't, I tried to leave her alone, and I told her to move on. Looks like she did what I told her to do, now I need to live with it. But how?

Watching her dance tonight with him is killing me. That fucker between my legs won't stop tormenting me tonight either. I may be a pussy, but he is hot on the trail, like a fucking beacon, finding her in the crowd and aiming right at her, the damn thing has no shame. But she is so wild tonight, her dancing has taken on a new level of sexy. She is giving me as good as she has ever got from my exploits with other women, she is punishing me, and it hurts, bad.

Is this how she felt all those times she saw me with other women? No wonder my brothers were so mad at me, I was destroying her if she felt it even a fraction of how I feel it now. Why did she have to be Joker's sister? Why couldn't she have been some random chick? I'll always love her, but I'll never have her. Fuck.

We're almost done one more song. Then I am going to talk to her, tell her not to sleep with this man if she hasn't already. I'm going to ask her to be careful, take her time. Don't do this to punish me, just wait for the right man.

But when I start the song, I look up to see her leading him out of the bar, they are leaving. And if the look on his face and hers says anything, it says sex. She is going home with him. Oh god, no Trinity, don't go, I say to myself, willing her to stay. But she goes, and as I watch her walk out of Mother's with him, I feel my heart shatter, I know it will never be the same again, watching my very heart walk out of the bar to go home with another man.

Chapter Four

Trinity:

"Good, all set then. Sunday picnic, Sunday night party, Monday rest and relaxation!" I say. I am so excited! A beach party and picnic, it's been a while since we've had a beach party, and we need to do it now since the season will be over soon. Lake Meade is perfect this time of year. The rest of the country may be getting ready for fall, but in Vegas, we swim and have mild temperatures all the way to Thanksgiving.

I am not oblivious to Pipe's obvious discomfort at me telling everyone I'd go help him pick out a good spot at the cove for us. Oh well, he needs to get over it. I am going to dance while everyone is here, and the music is blasting out and the beer is flowing!

My dad, T-Man, and my mom are sitting in a booth arguing while Pipes is sitting at the bar with a bottle of Southern Comfort and a shot glass. I know I am the reason my parents are arguing. They hate my bold clothing and my obvious desire to attract a man from the MC. Mom is wanting me excluded from club events, Dad won't keep me from the club now that I am twenty-two he feels I have a right to make my own mistakes.

Then there is Pipes, a lone sour-faced man drinking shots at the bar, looking anywhere but at me. I am dancing with a group of six or seven men. Trying to pick out which one is worthy of my time.

Snake is over with Rory at the bar, talking to Pipes, they keep looking over at me and I know they are talking about me, well tough. If he wanted me, he should have fought for me. Now it's too late and I'm going to find a man for me.

"Hey, can I cut in?" Joker says.

"Bro, I'm dancing with a MAN, do you really want to sister dance now?" I ask in exasperation.

But, the man who was closest, and making my shortlist, got the message and kissing my hand he walks away.

"So, Joker, how old do I have to be before you stop cock-blocking all the men I want to be with?"

"Sixty or so, but only if they are worthy."

"I guess I need to go somewhere else."

"Dad and mom would prefer that. You know they don't want you with a brother sis."

"Why? If the MC lifestyle is good enough for them, for you, then why not me?"

"You know that mom doesn't like the lifestyle. Why do you think dad spends time at Pin Stripes and is rarely at the clubhouse? Why do you think mom rarely attends functions? She hates it."

"Why Joker? Do you have some idea?" I ask.

"Yeah, dad told me once when I asked him why he never came to the parties as Ranger does."

"Well?" I ask, again.

"When they were young before we were born, mom caught dad with a club whore. She nearly left him and it was a real problem, for years. That's when he stopped taking runs and started Pin Stripes. After that he only did charity runs to get his miles in each year, no more pipeline or protection runs, nothing. It was that or lose mom," Joker explains.

"Wow, hard to see our dad as a man-whore," I laugh.

"I doubt he was that bad. I guess he just had a sweet butt that he'd had a bit before mom, then after mom the bitch didn't want to let go. Dad got drunk at a party and she climbed on. Mom came looking for him, found him on a couch, bitch riding him, and she pulled the bitch off him, threw her wedding ring at him, and left. She went to grandma's in Maine and it took him two months to get her to even talk to him."

"I guess that explains a lot about moms club attitude."

"Yeah, and they are not blind Trinity. They know the man you want, and they also know he IS a man-whore. Mom is trying to protect you from that hurt."

"I know, but Joker, I've tried. I can't forget him. I want to, every time I come here, he breaks my heart with the whores, yet I can't move on, god knows I've tried. Then he'll kiss me, or do something possessive and I am back to square one. That's why I haven't been here much lately. It's not mom, it's me, avoiding him."

"Aw sweetheart, want me to kill him? Then you won't ever have to see him again," Joker hugs me close as he utters those words that are only part teasing.

"Nope, I don't get to have him, but I don't want to be in a world that he doesn't exist in," I tell him. Then, looking towards the bar, I realize he is gone. I look around just in time to see him leaving the bar, his arm around a sweet butt, Jazmin. I need out of here.

"I have to go, Joker, I should not have come. I'll be at the party at the Lake, then I need to avoid the club. I don't think I will get my bad boy biker after all. I need to find a bad boy in another place, maybe a fighter, or a cop even. No musicians and no bikers."

"You ok to ride?"

"Yeah, I only had one beer. Besides, I need to clear my head. I think I'll ride to Calico Ridge and star gaze for a few hours. I have my sleep bag in my saddlebag."

"Trinity, I don't like you going out there alone."

"I know, but I need some alone time. I need a plan brother dear, time to find another life. This one hurts too bad." Then I kiss him and walk out. I'm going to have to leave for real soon. I know it, I've just been putting off the inevitable.

The next night I go to Rage after helping Pipes find a spot for the picnic the next day. I planned to stay overnight and maybe talk a bit, like when we were friends. We'd sit at Calico Ridge and watch the stars, sleeping under them once or twice. That is why I have to go there alone now, it was our spot. Pipes asked me to leave the lake, not stay overnight. So, here I am. I'll dance, see what the night holds.

"Hey, Trin, what's up? Did you and Pipes find a good spot? Rory asks.

"Yeah, he is staying out there tonight to be sure that no one gets the spot, then we are going out super early to set up."

"You sound bad, what happened with Pipes now?"

"He didn't want me to stay overnight, said he had some company coming out later, I know what that means."

"Come on girl, it's break time, let's cut loose and dance a bit." Rory drags me to the dance floor. Rory is the dancer extraordinaire. She is going to start a dance studio one day. We are on the dance floor, shaking and grinding but we don't dance for long when a man from the San Diego group, Treat, cuts in on us and asks me to dance.

Treat is one super-hot man, tattooed entirely, I doubt he has a visible spot available other than his face, and he is tall enough that even at five-nine with my spiked heels I am still a couple of inches shorter than he is. Complete that picture with nice muscles, blond curly hair, and a sweet as sugar smile, hm, I do like what I am grinding against now.

Snake comes up to rescue Rory from her solitary dance now that I have a partner. The dance is slow, so I clearly hear when he tells her that Pipes will blow a gasket. My girl Rory sticks up for me though with her response.

"Good, he's hurt her too much."

31

"Rory, he does love her," Snake answers.

Treat dances me away from the couple so I don't hear any more. But that's ok, I'm basking in the attention of this fascinating man in my arms.

Pipes:

I am sitting out here, alone, staring up at the stars and thinking about Trinity. I hurt her again tonight, implied that I had a girl coming out to be with me. Liar. I just can't be alone with her or I will take her. My cell phone buzzes and I see Snake is texting me.

Snake: Man what did you say to Trinity tonight?

Pipes: Why, what's wrong?

Snake: She's at Rage, dancing with Treat and he is eating her alive.

Pipes: Fuck, send me a pix

Snake: four pix coming

And I see her dancing with him, then walking to a couch where she is on his lap, then FUCK, she is straddling his lap.

Pipes: Get her the FUCK out of there Snake, without Treat.

Snake: How do I do that? Any real ideas?

Pipes: BEG

Pipe's Dream

I continue to text Snake to find out what Trinity is doing with Treat.

Snake: fuck that brother, I love Trinity too

Pipes: she can't hook up with a brother man.

Snake: he is from SD, she could move there.

Pipes: Get her off him!

Snake: Nope, looks like she will finally get that itch scratched brother.

Pipes: FUCK, I'm on my way.

I go ahead and load up in my truck, planning to go to Rage and get her. But, before I get to the main road, my phone beeps. I look down and see that I've got another text.

Snake: She left man, with Treat.

I don't answer, I can't. All I can think is that I need to see if she went to her apartment. I'll drive by there first. If she's not there I'm heading to the clubhouse to be sure she isn't there with Treat. If he touches her, I'll kill him.

I drive by her house, but no lights are on, and no bike out front. I knock on her door and no one answers. I head to the clubhouse, and immediately I see Treat's bike. I go into the clubhouse and looking around I don't see him. Then, I go into the playhouse and see he is there, bent over a blond and pounding away. I see red! I go to the man and pulling him off the blond I

33

am ready to knock him out when I see it is Candy he is pummeling, not Trinity.

"Fuck, man, what is your problem."

"Where is Trinity?" I shout.

"What? At home I guess, we parted in the lot at Rage man. She's Ranger's niece, I'm not tapping that," he says.

"Fuck,"

"Can I get back to Candy? Or do you still want to pound me?"

"Carry on," I say, then I leave, heading back to the lake.

Trinity:

The day at the lake was tedious, I wish I'd found some way to avoid the entire day. The tension was high between Pipes and me and some little kiddo nearly drowned in the lake, but our boys, Snake especially, saved him.

And, if that wasn't the worse part, the shit went south with the San Diego club and now we are arguing about confinement and lockdown.

"Dad, why?" I ask.

"There is no need for you to stay here the entire time, just when you are not at work. A prospect can follow you otherwise.

34

The problem isn't about you anyway, it's about Rory, we just don't know if anyone else will be hit in the crossfire." Dad says.

The men left, and Rory and I started dancing, in the bar, having some drinks and just having fun. Rory and I made a real connection. I loved partying with her. She was starting to act and feel like an old lady. She makes Snake so happy. I am thrilled my best friend has a woman worthy of him.

Rory had inked her entire leg with a property stamp. I showed her my back, which was inked with a full back of angel wings, warrior style, and the Road Warriors patch within the wings. She was fascinated. I see another tat in her future.

The bar closed for the night, we helped lock up, called the prospects who met us at the door, and headed to the clubhouse where a few of the other women were waiting for the guys to return. When we arrived, the clubhouse was busy for this time of night. Josie and Penny had gone home, but Cat was still here, although she was already in bed with her daughter Lissey. Christy was playing pool with another sweet butt, Candy, and Trinity and I decided to have a couple of drinks and dance a bit more before going to bed. The prospects that had been guarding the clubhouse came in for a break and the two that had been with Trinity and I were now outside on the gate and the perimeter.

We put on the music, soft dance music and we drank a couple of shots, then we started to dance, and as usual, as the music takes over we lose ourselves in the music, dancing and swaying and not aware of the world around us until the pop, pop, pop of gunfire is heard ringing throughout the clubhouse.

"Oh my god!" I scream.

35

"Get down!" Rory shouts to everyone and no one.

"Candy, oh my god are you ok?" Christy is screaming and looking down at a blood-soaked Candy, who even from across the room it is obvious that she is dead. A pool of dark blood is pooling from under her body. The man that had been inside guarding the clubhouse is down and bleeding and not moving.

Six men come into the clubhouse, three of them I know – too well, and the others I've never seen before. The men come in and pull Christy, Rory, and me away from the bar, handcuffing us all and taking us out and pushing us into a van.

"What do you want with us?" I scream.

The guy who seems to be in charge turns to Rory, and with a leer starts talking to her.

"Aurora, babe you know exactly what I want," Ripper says. "Now hush and be still and your friends won't get hurt."

We pull away and I'm wondering what happened to the other prospects. I lay down on the floor of the van, softly crying and wondering how it all went to shit so quickly.

Pipes:

When we heard that the clubhouse had been hit, I felt my stomach clench. Trinity, god, what if she'd been hurt? Ranger tells us that there are three missing people; Rory, Trinity, and Christy. Everyone else was in bed and apparently once they found Rory, they didn't go any further." Ranger concluded.

36

"Fuck!" Snake yells, running to his bike to take off. I followed him, feeling desperate at the thought of Trinity in those men's hands. Joker looks at his dad, then follows us out the door also following us to ensure we make it there safely.

When we reach the clubhouse, the police had already been there and left. I didn't even take the time to put down my kickstand on my bike, I just dumped it and ran into the clubhouse. Seeing Wicked, who was on perimeter watch, I grabbed him up and nearly beat the shit out of him before I was pulled off of him.

"How the fuck did this happen?" I scream at him.

"Man, they had our cuts, when they got close enough for me to see the SoCal rocker It was too late, they shot me in the arm then hit me over the head. When I came to it was over." Wicked said. I could tell the man was upset, but I couldn't deal with it, not yet.

Ranger immediately posted a full contingent of guards, called in allies including our charter club in Pahrump and several in Arizona and Utah. Leaders of all the Western clubs were called and the situation in San Diego was discussed far and wide.

For now, that's all we can do, Neither Trinity nor Rory had cell phones with them, and if Christy has one, no one knows the number for tracing. She was only a sweet butt, not someone that the brothers keep track of. In essence, we are at a standstill.

I look over to the sound of Charlotte crying. She is leaning against Joker, sobbing that her innocent baby girl is in the hands of rapists. I hear Joker confirming with his mom that Trinity is still a virgin, so, people are flipping out at her kidnapping.

Still a virgin? What about that fucking college man? That Gregg guy she went home with? Was she still holding out? Waiting for me?

I understand how her family is upset, but I am so freaked out. I just can't control my rage. I don't give a fuck if I'm showing my feelings, fuck it. I can't deal with this, I need to find her. I take off to ride, needing to do something, even if it's wrong. Running to my bike, I take off, ending up at Calico Ridge, I hear the other bike, so I know I have an escort. But, whoever it is they are wise enough to stay back and not intrude. I'd have to kick their ass, this is a special place, mine and Trinity's place, I can't have intrusions. I sit on the ground, upset, looking to the starts and it isn't until I settle that I realize I have tears trailing down my face.

Trinity:

Once they take us out of the van and into the dilapidated cabin. Our kidnappers start talking to Rory like old friends.

"So, Aurora looks like we got you some company. Who are your friends?" Ripper asks.

"Trinity is T-Man's daughter, Ranger's niece. You should have left her there Jamey, I'm nothing to the club, but she is family."

"Well, at the meeting they claimed you were family too, so, we'll see." He says.

"Ripper, brother, I want one of them for my own." The one called Shackle says.

"We will see brother, we will see."

38

"What about you?" he asks, pointing to Christy.

"No one will pay you for me, she says. I'm just a sweet butt." There is total defeat in her voice, knowing she isn't valuable to the club.

"Well then, we know what your job will be don't we?" Ripper says.

"Just don't hurt me and I'll cooperate," she says.

"Boys, here's your reward, take it easy on her if you want her to last," Ripper says, and three of the men take Christy to a back room and it is easy to hear the sexual noises of the men getting started. I look at Rory and she looks at me.

"Trinity is worth more to you intact, unhurt, Jamey. Her family will do anything, pay anything to get her back. But if you hurt her they will hunt you down until they find and kill you." Rory tells him.
"Maybe she'd be worth it," he says.

"And maybe she won't," Rory says.

"Well for now I am only interested in getting you back and into my bed again. Then your boy toy will leave you alone since I've reclaimed you. He won't want you once I've taken you again."

"Just please Jamey, let Trinity go home. She isn't part of this and she isn't a whore. She has someone that cares about her and she needs to go home."

"Tell you what, I'll let her go, unhurt, now, if you agree to back my claim and stay with me until I am tired of you." He is looking her dead in the eyes. I know he means it. He will only let me go if Rory agrees to stay with him.

"Fine, call her dad, let her go and I'll go on with you." She tells him.

"Rory don't," I beg her.

"Snake will not be able to handle losing you," I tell her.

"Trinity, I have to. I will not let you be hurt over me. Pipes will never get over it, you know that. And trust me, it isn't something you want to live with either. Just go home and promise me, you'll tell Snake I am sorry, but that I have to finish this. Our timing just wasn't right," she tells me.

"Aw, how sweet. Now, let me see if the boys are done, and you will give me a sample of how cooperative you are going to be, then we'll call her folks and tell them where she is, we'll be long gone before they get here to get her."

They go into the bedroom, leaving me tied to a chair in the front room. I hear the sounds of sex coming from that room and I know they are raping Rory, again.

When they finish and are preparing to leave, Rory comes to me and gives me a quick hug and tells me to go home. Everything will be ok.

Pipe's Dream

Pipes:

I felt the vibration of my cell phone, just before dawn. Ranger texted me GPS coordinates where Trinity was being left behind, in good faith, since Rory agreed to cooperate and go with them on her own.

The ride to the location where Trinity is being held is harrowing, I wasn't with the group, since I was already near Lake Las Vegas on the way out of town when they sent me the coordinates. Even though I was a bit ahead of them, no one was following the speed limits and we are all just trying to get there fast.

I saw the guys as I pulled into the entrance to the campground and I followed them to a cabin where I saw other bikes stopping. Several brothers were inside the cabin and I didn't even stop when my bike came to a stop, I dumped it and ran into the cabin calling out for Trinity. She was in her father's arms, but when she heard me she jumped up and ran to me.

She launched herself towards me, I caught her up and she wrapped her legs around my waist and buried her face in my neck as she began to cry.

"Shh, now Trinity, it's ok girl. Did he hurt you, sweetheart?" I asked her in a soothing tone, rubbing her hair.

"Trinity, did he hurt you?" more strongly this time.

"No, Rory stopped them," she cried, then her next words confirmed to me the magnitude of what had happened.

"Pipes, she traded herself for me, they hurt her instead."

41

Raven Featherwood

She continued to sob, holding me tighter as Ranger and her dad walked closer to us. It was almost as though she feared they'd take her away from me.

"Trinity, honey I know you are upset but I need to know, what happened to Christy and Rory?" Ranger asked.

She turned in my arms to look at her uncle. Then with a sad look at me, she answered.

"Christy told them she wouldn't be ransomed since she wasn't claimed. So, the men, all of them, used her. I felt so bad for her. I wanted to tell her you'd pay to get her back daddy, but I didn't know if you would. And Rory, the man, Ripper, said he wasn't going to share her, and he took her to the room and raped her, they wouldn't call you to come to get me until she went into the room with them. Then when she came back, she didn't look at me, when I cried and got her attention she just said to go home. That she wouldn't let someone else get hurt on her account. Daddy her eyes were so scary, she looked blank, just blank."

Then she looked to Snake and god the pain in his eyes tore at me.

"Snake, she told him that every time he touched her she would be thinking of you, your hands, your body, your, well, everything. He got so mad at her that he told her he was letting his two friends have her once for her bad behavior. They didn't though before they left again anyway. So, I guess that would be later. Just before she left though she said to tell you she loved you and only you. Then they took her." Snake looked broken, he just stood there looking bleak with tears running down his face.

42

Pipe's Dream

Ranger had sent out several bikers in multiple directions to try to find their trail, but the rest of us had to head back to Vegas and take Trinity home.

She was insistent that she wanted to ride home with me, on my bike. So, even though her dad was NOT happy about it, I gave her my helmet, and tucked her onto my bike, pulling her tight against my back.

(Following week)

Trinity was a wreck when she got home. She feels responsible for Rory going with the men and she isn't handling it too well. Her mother, Charlotte, took her away on an extended vacation in Maine, where she can relax and try to come to terms with her abduction. Charlotte's mother, Rena, lives in a quaint little town in Maine on the coast with rocky beaches and majestic forests. Plus she has a doting grandmother to give her lots of love and comfort.

One of the reasons that T-Man and Charlotte hurried this trip away and wanted Trinity to leave was the hope that the time away would help her to settle her nerves, and maybe overcome this fascination she seems to have with me. Her dad made it clear to me that he didn't approve. Unfortunately, her parents, especially her father, are well aware of my reputation as a man-whore and they are sure I will only hurt their baby girl.

Chapter Five

Rory (three months later):

My time here has been rejuvenating. I love my grandmother, and her home here in Maine is beautiful and peaceful. Mom didn't stay more than a couple of days, then she went back home. I spent most of my time going to farmer's markets, touring local farms, and riding horses.

Rory was finally found and brought home. Snake and the men took care of the men that took us, but, even after talking to Rory on the phone, I wasn't ready to go home. I needed time to get over Pipes and decide what I would do with the rest of my life.

Mom and dad are not going to let me date him, and they are not about to let me date any other brother, so I need to decide if I want to find another man, or if I want to go to a different MC for a visit to find a biker from a different club.

I did talk to Pipes a couple of times, he was concerned, even worried. But he never really asked me to come home or to be part of his life. I can't go back to being in love with a man that is not my own.

I decide to go over to my grandmother's sitting room and talk to her. Whenever I've had issues that I can't resolve, my grandmother has been a good sounding board. And she loves to talk about men!

"Grandmother are you around?" I call out.

"Yes dear, I'm here, come on in."

Pipe's Dream

"Can you talk? I have some things I'd like to ask you."

"Of course, sweetheart, ask away."

"There is a man, grandmother. A man in mom and dad's MC. I've known him since high school and he and I used to be good friends."

"How good?" she asked.

"Good enough, I'm still a virgin grandmother, so not too good," I smirked.

"Well, what happened?"

"He took me to prom, we made out a bit, and the chemistry was off the charts. Then, the next day, poof. He wanted nothing to do with me, not even our friendship."

"Baby that was years ago, are you still pining for this same boy?"

"Yes. Grandmother, I love him. I've always loved him, and I'm afraid I always will."

"Oh dear, what do your parents think of him?"

"They love him as an MC brother, but they don't approve of him. He's a biker, you know how mom feels about the MC, they won't let me date one."

"Well, you are an adult now, you can do what you want."

"Not in the MC, dad and Uncle Ranger made me off-limits, so none of the men in the MC will even touch me."

"Las Vegas is a big town, you can find men in other places."
"Well, see, I'm kind of a biker bitch," I say with a wince. "I love that biker image, the big bad boys with ink and muscles. I'm not attracted to other kinds of men. Believe me, I've tried."

"Hmm, maybe it's a change of venue you need. Ever thought about going to another city for a year or two?"

"No, but maybe I should."

"You could stay here."

"No offense Grandmother, but I like the City too much to move to the country."

"Well, a different City then. You may just need to get away from all that is familiar and see what else is out there. You will most likely not get over him watching him daily. Give it some time, if you still love him. Then fight for him. It sounds to me like your young man is trying to honor your parent's wishes, and is as attracted to you as you are to him, otherwise why run away after the prom?"

"I think he feels it too, when they found me, in that cabin, he was so intense. He didn't care that my dad and brother was right there, he grabbed me, held me, and made me stay with him all the way home."

"Hm, sounds like a man in love."

"I hope so, but if he can't make a decision, I have to."

"I'm afraid so sweetheart, life is too short to spend it pining on a man you'll never have."

"Thanks, I think I'm going to go home. Confront him, then if it isn't going to happen, I'll take your advice. I'll leave."

Chapter Six

Pipes:

She is coming home. Everyone is getting together this weekend for a welcome home party. I can't wait to see her, know that she is ok. But I shouldn't even go to that party. I will just torture myself, again.

I think I am going to take a run, out of town for this weekend. Not be here for the party, avoid this issue. Yeah, I'll call Ranger tomorrow and talk to him about a run.

After Ranger heard I was interested in getting out of town this weekend, and knowing he was aware of the tension between Trinity and myself, he sent me to the Washington chapter to check on some things to do with the pipeline set up and so I packed my saddlebags and left first thing, not even waiting for her to get in.

Trinity:

The party was fun, I danced and had a good time, but I missed Pipes. He didn't even show up. When I asked Fox where he was, he told me that Ranger had sent him to Washington. I can't believe that he sent him away, right when I came home. I don't know when I'll see him, but with Snake and Rory's wedding coming up, I hope I see him soon. I have told myself that if he doesn't make his move by then, I would leave.

(Two weeks later)

Pipe's Dream

I cannot believe this amazing studio! Rory has outdone herself, I never expected it to be this big, and all the rooms, set up for different types of dancing. I'd love to learn salsa dancing. I've never seen anyone dance like Rory. I am a dancing fool, but Rory is dance personified.

We are all setting up to learn pole dancing. I've been drinking, but that is fine. We have a line of cabs setting up out front at two am, so I don't care if I am drunk. My bike is at home since I rode over with Cat, and Fox is picking her up. I can always ride home with them if I need to. So, bottoms up!

Oh lord, look at that outfit!

"Wow Rory, what a sex kitten outfit. Too bad your man isn't here to see that! You should take that one homegirl." I say, looking at Rory all dolled up.

"Yeah, he would like the whole peasant look too." Rory answers.

"What kind of outfits do you have for all of us," Cat asks.

"Come look, there are lots of neat clothes, just try some till you like one."

"I brought my own, Christy says."

"Well I didn't," I say, going to look through the stripper clothes.

I found a sexy crochet outfit and coverup, and then I put on some sexy heels, let down my hair and teased it up some, put on bright red lipstick, and sauntered into the room.

"Hell yeah Trinity!" Cat says. "You look hot". So, let's dance ladies!

Rory goes over to the sound system and puts on a sexy song that she then proceeds to show us all her pole dancing skills. And damn, that woman has skills!

"Girl, where did you learn that?" Cat asks.

"You go girl," Trinity says, "now teach baby teach."

We go to the poles and dance until we are exhausted. Then after another drink, some munchies, and a rest Cat gets up and tells us to put on a performance. She asks us all to take to our poles, she puts on a playlist for stripping, then she puts on the disco ball and kills the other lights. She was dancing, but the pole was challenging for her, she's six months pregnant so she was playing around, but mostly watching.

Suddenly I look around, feeling him, knowing he was there, and watching, I see the room is full of the men from Snake's party. Fox is standing with his arms around Cat, who is grinning like a Cheshire cat. I knew she did this.

I look around to see Pipes, he is standing right in front of me. I love the heat I see in his eyes. Good. It's time the man made up his mind.

Pipes:

What the Fuck! We walked into the dance studio expecting to find all the women drinking and dancing and acting foolish. What we didn't expect was to walk in and find them all in slinky stripper clothes and pole dancing.

Pipe's Dream

My eyes immediately found Trinity. Dressed in a slinky string bikini that was three triangles of crocheted fabric held together by crocheted strings, she had six-inch stiletto heels, and a masque, hiding her face did nothing for the fact that all these men could see every other part of her sexy body as she worked the fuck out of that pole. Where in the shit did she learn to move like that, and her still a virgin!

I didn't even think, I just walked straight up to her and as soon as I got her attention and she saw me, I was dragging her off that pole and into my arms, I turned and walked out of that room, away from all the gawking eyes and into an empty room.

"Trinity, what the fuck woman, where are your clothes?" I say breathlessly. I need to not touch her again. Holding her near-naked form in my arms nearly killed me. My fucking dick is so hard it is like it is on a homing beacon aimed straight to her.

"Hey Pipes baby," she says drunkenly. "How are you doing? Where is your whore of the day hot stuff, did you forget her somewhere, or are you heading back to the clubhouse to get her?"

"Don't Trinity," I say to her, knowing this is her way of deflecting from her nudity.

"Why not Pipes, those are the women you like, so I don't understand why you are here cock blocking me. There were bound to be some men in there that would have liked me. And then I wouldn't have to be lonely and horny."

"Trinity, baby stop. You know I care about you, want you. I just can't claim you baby."

51

"Whatever," she says.

"No Trinity, not whatever. I want you, I have wanted you since you were in high school, but your dad and mom have made it clear, no bikers. And baby, you deserve something much more than a biker with no future." I tried to explain it to her.

"I've tried for years to find someone else, someone that isn't a biker isn't you. I thought I'd found someone in Gregg, but then he saw us together and realized I still loved you, so he left me too. I'm just not good enough for anyone." She was turning sad and crying now.
"It isn't that baby, you are too good for us. Way too good." I said, running my hands over my face.

"No, Paul." She said, calling me by my real name, something she never did. "I see you with all the women, you give them all of you, I can't get anything from you, and I actually love you. They just want to be a biker's old lady, they don't love the man like I do."

"You don't love me, baby, you only think that you do. When you meet the right man, you'll know it. But Trinity, baby I will always love you, only you. Those women Trinity, they are a release, a way to forget for a minute that I can't have you. But, know this woman, my heart, it is yours and only yours it has been since you were seventeen and rode on my bike."

"You love me? But won't claim me, won't have me? Why the fuck not?"

"Because you are too good Trinity, you need a man that can give you a nice home, children and a life full of PTA meetings, picnics, vacations, and peace. I'm not that man baby."

"Can't you just love me this once? Can't I have one night to remember forever? I don't want my first time to be with someone I don't love I want it to be you."

"No, Trinity I can't touch you, baby. If I do I won't be able to let you go." I tell her.

"Well fuck you then!" she screams at me.

"Trinity please." I try to calm her.

"NO! I'll be gone tomorrow, I won't bother you again Paul Jennings, I will leave you to your fucking whores and lonely life. Be a fucking martyr then, be alone. I am leaving, and I will find someone to fuck ME instead of a whore. Now get the fuck away from me. I am done loving you."

I was stunned, I just stood there watching as she walked out of the room, grabbing a dressing robe she wrapped that beautiful body up and went right out the door and to the waiting row of cabs that had been arranged to take the women home. I'd give her the night to sober up, tomorrow morning I'd go talk to her, make her understand that I do love her. Then, if she really wants me, we'll go talk to her parents and they'd just have to understand and accept that she was going to have to be a biker's woman.

Having made up my mind to claim her, I went back to my room at the clubhouse, and after showering and changing my sheets to get rid of the scents of past conquests, I laid down to sleep off the party and prepare for the next day, when I'd go claim my woman.

Chapter Seven

Trinity:

I watched as the lights of the city faded behind me. I was sober now that I'd cried, showered, and made some plans. Dressed in my jeans, black tank, and my RWMC Angels Warrior cut, with the Angel of T-Man on the back, I had my saddlebags packed with several changes of clothes, one nice dress-up outfit, and one sexy outfit, I'd pulled together some necessary items into a backpack and my cash in my tummy purse, my 38 special in my shoulder holder and my knives in the ankle holsters. I was leaving Las Vegas, without a destination in mind.

I was a fucking grown-ass woman and it was time I headed out into the world and made myself a life. I'd left a note for my mom and dad, one for Snake, one for Cat, and one for Lissey. Other than that, I was out of here and everyone could fuck off. I'd be back when I decided I was ready.

I headed North, it was summer, and the weather was good, I'd ride to Utah, head over to Colorado, and from there well, we'd see. The Boulder Chapter of the RWMC had some damn fine men, and they were family-oriented like our chapter was, not a bunch of badasses. So, I figured I'd be safe enough there and it would give me a couple of weeks downtime to decide what to do.

I know that Uncle Ranger will know where I am, no one is going to house me, in a clubhouse, and not tell the President of the Mother Chapter that I am there. That was fine, but I wasn't going to allow them to treat me like a glass doll either, and if I couldn't get treated decent, I'd stop hanging at the clubhouses and I'd go rogue.

My phone rang constantly, often it was Pipes calling and texting, he even tried bribing me with text messages saying he wanted to claim me and for me to please come home. Even that he'd already decided before I'd left that he was going to talk to my parents, I call bull shit. I was damn near naked in his presence begging him to spend a night with me and he'd turned me away, telling me I'd know when I met the right man. So, fuck him, I'm on the hunt.

I don't answer any calls except my dad. He called and said that Pipes had gone to my house and had found my notes. He'd read them all I guess and had called my dad and mom. It didn't matter, my mind was made up.

"Trinity, sweetheart, come home so we can sort this ok?" dad asked.

"Nope, it is time I saw some of the other club's daddy, decide if I want the MC life or not before settling for something else."

"Trinity, I am so sorry you feel you'd be settling. Your mom and I just wanted you to have options, not just the club that you'd grown up with."

"I see, so you made all the eligible men, including Paul, think I was off-limits forever, so I could have options?" I scoffed at him with that comment.

"Yes, we wanted you to date other kinds of men."

"Well, I was a fool. I fell for a biker that follows orders. Now, I need to follow my way to see if it is a biker that I need to get over him, or if I can live a life outside the club. And dad, I will figure it out. Then, maybe I'll settle somewhere else, or maybe I'll come home. I'm not sure yet."

"I will withdraw my orders about you then, Pipes can date you, see if it works out."

"Too little too late daddy, he doesn't want me. That man turned me down flat, and I was near naked at the time."

"Trinity, what are your plans? You can't just ride your bike all over the place. What about a place to stay? Money? Come on girl this is not a good idea." Dad tells me, getting angry but trying to contain it so I don't hang up.

"Dad, I have some savings, when it gets low I'll find a job in a bar or diner or something until I have enough to move on. When I meet Mr. Right, I'll know and settle." I tell him.

"Trinity you are nuts! Listen, at least stay in the clubhouses, it will lend you some protection and give you a free place to stay, will you do that for me?" He asks.

"Ok, daddy, I'll stay as long as Uncle Ranger doesn't make everyone treat me like a baby angel with a broken fucking wing," I say.

"I'll talk to him. You won't be treated like you are off-limits, but you will NOT be treated as a club whore either, do you understand me, girl? Remember that you do represent this club and this family when you go to the clubhouses. And your mom and I will supplement your money until you decide what you are going to do, we'll make regular deposits. I don't need to worry that you are working in a dive for pennies and not eating well or having to stay in a bad situation because you can't afford to leave."

"Thank you, daddy. I'd appreciate that and pay you back when I settle."

"Trinity have you considered going to Maine more permanently? If you don't want to be here honey?"

"Nope already spent months there, ended up coming home to give him one last chance and he blew it. So now I have to find Mr. Right, and since only bikers come into my life in Vegas, I'm looking elsewhere."

I knew my dad was frustrated, but I agreed to stay at clubhouses where I could, to call weekly, accept the money they would deposit, and to be careful. I mean what else could they do, I am twenty-two years old and free to do as I please.

Pipes:

She is gone, again. She left before I could get to her to explain. She won't respond to my texts, she won't accept my calls, and she won't tell anyone, including her dad where she is going. I've lost her, and it is my own fucking fault.

I sat with her mom and dad and explained the past few years. How hard we've tried to stay away from each other and how I've loved her since we were kids but I stayed away to respect their wishes. Her mom was the most upset, going on about me and my whores and how her daughter deserved fidelity and all. T-Man stopped her though, especially when I looked at him and told him I was trying to forget her and trying to run her off, so she'd find a good man.

It didn't matter, Joker came in and was furious that she'd left. I told him about the night before, and what happened at the dance studio. He just looked at me. Then without another word walked out.

I told her dad if I found her, I was claiming her and if they didn't approve or accept it then we'd leave and go to another chapter. Or, if it took it, we'd leave the MC completely. He was surprised I would say that because that is when he stood up and called Joker back into the house.

"Joker get the fuck in here, now." T-Man said to his son who was standing out back, talking on his phone to someone.

"Char, I want you to stay in here for this discussion, but, if you cannot be agreeable and fair then leave the room." He told his wife. She chose to stay but she looked anything but happy.

As Joker came running into the room, looking for what had his dad so upset, he looked to me and then his father, and I know he was wondering if he would get to knock me out.

"What dad?" Joker asked, again looking to me like I was the threat.

"Your sister is going to make a big mistake if we don't find a way to stop her. I am accepting Pipe's claim on her, as of now. I will let Ranger know so if any clubs contact us he can inform them. I want you and Pipes to pack up for a run. You will go together and find her. We will pass on any info we have on her to you, so you can trace her steps. She is a day ahead of you two, so you need to get moving."

"Dad? Pipes has claimed her, and you are ok with this?" He asks.

"Fuck yeah, he has tried to respect our wishes, and now instead of being here with someone who honestly loves her, she is traipsing all over the place looking for a substitute. Fuck knows she is a damn fine-looking woman, away from us, she'll be claimed before we know it and by someone not half as good for her as Pipes."

I jump up to head to the clubhouse.

"I can be ready within the hour," I tell Joker. "Do you have any idea which way she headed when she left?" I ask T-Man.
"Geek is looking into her bank account. She filled up her tank last night in Mesquite, so we know she headed North into Utah. That's all we have so far, she must have cash too because there have been no other purchases on her card since that fill up. Also, we talked to the Utah and Wyoming charters and they are watching for her. California and Colorado have also been notified. We have to watch and wait. We do know North was the last direction, so head North and we'll let you know when we find anything else. Phones on vibrate and against your chest while you ride." He tells us.

"Got it, Joker, meet me at the clubhouse?"

"Yeah brother, be there in a few."

And that is how I find myself in Salt Lake City, with Joker, at the RWMC clubhouse, trying to settle my nerves with whiskey and for the first time, fending off the club whores having no desire to touch anyone but Trinity again.

Pipe's Dream

Trinity: (four days later):

Instead of going to Colorado, I decided that I had enough cash and the weather was so good I'd just ride the medicine bow mountains and have some quiet time, alone. I rode through some of the most beautiful places in the country, and I had solitude to find my peace, a peace that I'd been missing for quite a while.

This would be my last night in Wyoming. I'd gone East and found myself in Laramie where there isn't an RWMC charter, but several good ole boy country-western bars. After finding a small quaint motel that didn't look too seedy, I took a shower, changed into clean jeans and a more conservative tee and my cut, I put my Harley boots back on and put my cash in the safe, leaving about fifty in my pocket, along with my ID and I went to the closest bar to have a few beers and see what kind of fun I could have.

Before going to drink, I turned my phone on and sent a text to my dad, I told him I was fine and I'd be heading to a charter clubhouse the next day. I'd decided to go North then East to Rapid City where there was an established RWMC charter. I thought I'd spend a few days there, do laundry and sleep in a real bed. I'd camped in the mountains and while that was fun and peaceful, but I did miss the luxuries like hot water and a mattress.

As soon as I'd sent the text, I again turned off the phone. Saves batteries and keeps my location from being tracked. I'm not stupid, I know Geek could find me with my phone. So, even though they will know where I am once I hit the first clubhouse, I decided to take whatever time for myself that I could.

Going into the bar, I was surprised by the number of biker types that were in the place. It was a cowboy bar after all. I looked around and saw several handsome hot men in the place.

This has potential, I decided. I'd made a decision. There wasn't any sense in holding out for love with this virginity thing. I just needed someone to take it. I knew it would hurt and not feel good the first time, so I wanted to just get it over with and be done with it. Then, when I found a guy that I'd want, I wouldn't have to worry about the pain and the worry.

I went to the bar and ordered a beer, then turning to survey the bar I was taken by surprise when a good-looking man, who looked like he was in his mid-thirties sat beside me and started to hit on me.

"Hey, you just passing through, or did you come here on purpose Darlin?" He asked.

"Passing through, on my way to Rapid City," I say.

"What's in Rapid City? A man or family?" he asks.

"A Club," I say.

"A Club?"

"Yeah, Road Warriors MC, my family MC," I answer.

"I know that club, we have an MC here in Laramie, but they are not the Road Warriors. We are allies of a sort though. You alone?"

"Nope, I say, just grabbing a drink, then heading back to sleep before time to leave," I say.

"Well, would you like to dance before calling it a night?"

"Sure."

And heading to the dance floor, I find this man is a wonderful dancer, light on his feet, and wearing a Falcon MC cut that indicated he was a Road Captain. Now how did I miss that?

"So, you are in an MC too."

"Yep, noticed the cut huh?" he laughed.

"Yeah, so is your club a 1% club?" I ask.

"Naw, we are just a club of good ole boys and friends. One of our members is a local cop."

"Ok, then I can dance with you" I laugh. "I am not interested in any bikers that are into illegal shit."

"Whoa there filly, I'm not looking to marry up either, just a dance."

I start to laugh. Then I tell him what I am looking for, and the look on his face makes me chuckle.

"I've never had a woman proposition me like you just did girl. You just made my dick stand up without a touch or anything."

"Good, want to help a girl out?" I ask.

"Fuck yeah, where are you staying? Or do you want to come back to the clubhouse with me?" he asks.

"I'm just up the street, let's hit my room," I tell him. "But, grab a bottle, I need some liquid courage."

"You're on baby, let's go."

I find out his name is Marcus, but his road name is Hoop. I like the anonymity of the road name, so I call him Hoop. He asks me mine and I tell him, Angel, since I don't want to give him my real name. He also thinks I am from Rapid City, so I am again keeping it on the down-low. When we get to my motel room, we go in and I start removing my clothes immediately.

"You have condoms?" I ask.

"Sure do, now, let's have a drink and I'll make sure it's good for you." He says.

Drinking a serious shot of whiskey, right from the bottle, I go over to Hoop and standing up on my tippy toes, I kiss him. Before I know it, he has me in his arms and is kissing me back. I don't feel the knee melting hot chemistry that I feel from Pipes, but it doesn't feel bad either.

"Hmm, girl, your mouth is sweet, How does the rest of you taste, I wonder?" Hoop asks.

"Dunno, why don't you find out?"

Hoop laughs, deep in his throat, and picking me up he lays me onto the bed and undoing his belt he takes off his clothes, except for his boxers, and then pulling a condom out of his wallet, he lays it on the bed next to me and pulls my panties down and tosses them aside. Then, he looks at me with a hot look and asks me one last time if I am sure this is what I want. I tell him I am sure, then he lowers his head between my legs and begins to lick and kiss at my center, and all thought leaves me as this kind, handsome stranger makes love to me with his mouth, sending me into a sweet orgasm that almost makes me cry.

"God girl, you are amazing, and so responsive. I want you to cum again before I take you. I want you ready so it is good for you too." He says.

Then, he starts rubbing my clit with his one hand and using his finger he begins to finger fuck me until finally, he has two fingers in and I feel my hymen break as he plunges in until he reaches the end of his fingers and his hand is rubbing me, and he begins to push in and out, curling his fingers so they hit someplace inside me that sends me into another orgasm.

"Oh god, that feels so good." I cry out.

"Yeah, look at that beautiful virginal blood." He says, holding up his fingers which are coated in blood. "God must be smiling down on me today girl, you are a rare gift. I am going to enjoy fucking you until you are ruined for any dick but mine."

When Hoop says that, I realize that I've made a huge mistake. I don't want to be ruined. I want Pipes. And now I've given my virginity to a man that is not him. Fuck, what am I doing?

"Wait, Hoop, wait," I tell him.

"What Darlin? I am so ready to pop, I need inside you, or I am going to cum all over myself."

"Hoop, can I give you a blowjob instead?" I ask.

"Are you afraid? Having second thoughts? What?" he asks. "Yes, to all, can I get you off with a blow job?"

"Sure girl, you do that. Then, if you still want, I'll fuck you. I am good for three or four a night."

"Thank you, Hoop," I say, and getting on my knees in front of him I give the man a blow job worthy of all the YouTube and internet lessons I watched on the subject.

Following the blow job, we talked. I explained about Pipes, told him how I was looking for a place to settle and meet a good man to settle with. Hoop again said he wasn't going to settle at all, let alone with me. And, he suggested I save the real first time for a man that was. He broke me but hadn't fucked me, so I was still pure for a man in that respect.

Hoop kissed me tenderly, thanked me for the blow job, and left.

I showered, dressed, packed my bike, and left. I'd sleep tomorrow, tonight I needed to ride.

Pipes:

The phone was vibrating against my chest. It had been four days since we'd had any idea of where Trinity was. I was getting scared something had happened to her. I motioned to Joker to follow me and pulled over.

Pipe's Dream

"Yeah?" I answered

"We got a hit!" Geek said on the other end.

"Where?" I asked.

"Laramie Wyoming."

"We are not far from there, we were heading to Rapid City to wait for more info," I told Geek.

"We narrowed the cell signal down to a one-mile radius of a motel called the dusty tumbleweed. I'll text you the address."

"Thanks, man." And I told Joker what Geek had said, and we headed for Laramie.

When we got into Laramie and found the motel she'd called from, we were convincing enough that the desk clerk opened the door and we saw that she'd already left. But it wasn't hard to see that the bed had been used. The room smelled like sex, and a pair of lacy panties were laying just under the edge of the bed, Trinities scent, her perfume was in the room. Trinity had been here, and she'd had sex.

"Looks like she left already, too bad. The rooms paid for the night, so you can stay if you'd like." And then the desk clerk left us in the room.

Joker sat down on a chair, his head in his hands. I picked up the panties and sat on the edge of the bed. I could smell her, her sex, and I knew she'd been with a man. I was sick, and I stood suddenly going into the bathroom and threw up. This was all my fault. Then, splashing water in my face, I took the panties, that

67

were still in my hand. Putting them to my face, I inhaled. Then, stuffing them into my pocket. I went out and heading to the door, told Joker I was leaving.

"I saw a bar up the road, I need a drink." Then I went to my bike and rode to the bar.

Joker followed but I noticed he stopped outside the bar and was talking on the phone. I didn't wait. I just walked on in, went to the bar, and ordered two shots of Jack and a beer. Throwing back the shots, I started nursing the beer when I looked around the bar to see what kind of men were there and wondered if any of them had seen Trinity.

Just as Joker sat down, the bartender turned towards me and threw back over her shoulder to the man she was talking to, "Hoop has all the luck Thunder, you should hang by him. He hooked up with a beautiful out of town girl just a while ago. They danced one dance and left together. He must be magical to get her to leave after only one drink and one dance."

"Fucking lucky bastard. I saw that woman when she came in, riding a hot ass Harley too. I should have come in then, but I was called out to pick up a truck down on the highway, just got back."

"Love you Thunder, but Hoop is one hot ass man. She'd have picked him anyway."

"Thanks for that, now my ego is hurt." He answered.

I looked at the man Thunder and asked if Hoop was still here.

"Yeah, he was a while ago." Then looking around he pointed to a tall man over at the dartboard and said that Hoop was the one with the Falcon cut on. FUCK! A biker.

Joker grabbed my arm as I stood and started over to the dartboard. I shook him off and kept going.

"Damn, this isn't going to be good," Joker says.

"Why is he looking for Hoop?" the man, Thunder asked.

"That girl, the one you guys are talking about, that's his woman," Joker says following me across the bar.

I walk up to the man that is shooting darts with another, smaller man, and I call out to him.

"You Hoop?" I ask.

"Yeah, I'm Hoop." He answers and walks towards us, smiling.

"You know this woman?" I ask, holding up a photo of Trinity.

"Angel, yeah. She was here earlier tonight." Hoop said, looking at me intently, the smile gone.

"Where is she now?" I ask.

"I left her about an hour ago, she was in her motel room up the street. Why?"

I felt myself getting angry, and I knew I was about to lose my shit when the dumb fucker had to go and say something about Trinity that I couldn't take.

"She someone to you? She told me she was single and available man. She was just looking for a one-nighter, not anything else." Hoop said. Just before I nailed him a right hook to the face.

"Pipes stop man, not his fault. Back the fuck off before we lose her trail sitting in jail." Joker yells.

"You Pipes man?" Hoop asks, holding his jaw.

"Yes, why."

"Angel said she tried to get you to do her and you said no. So, she was looking for a fill-in man. Can't imagine anyone telling that gal no. Glad I got to meet you, punch, and all man. Couldn't imagine what a man that stupid would look like." Hoop said.

I was deflated. She'd even told the man I'd denied her? Fuck, I really did screw this up. I just sat down in the nearest chair and I know I was numb because I didn't even realize that Joker had come up with a drink for me until he lifted my hand and put it in my hand.

"Was she ok when you left her?" Joker asked.

"Yeah, but she was regretful. And although you don't deserve to hear this Pipes, I will tell you she backed out, changed her pretty little mind before I fucked her."

I heard that and looked up to the man, hopeful. Hoop killed that hope though with what he said next.

"But, I did get to taste that hot pussy of hers and give her two amazing orgasms and break her cherry with my hand before she backed out. Plus, you dumb mother fucker, she gave me the best damn blow job I've EVER had, and that is all on you for turning her away. Consider that my punch to your face." Hoop said before turning and walking away.

"Come on man, let's hit the road. We can be in Rapid City by morning and get some sleep there. Maybe Geek will have some more info for us by then." Joker told me.

I felt like I was sleepwalking as we left the bar. Hoops was right, and I couldn't blame him. What fucking man would say no to a beautiful girl like Trinity, who just wanted her virginity gone, and was offering a one-night stand with no strings attached? I was lucky as shit that the man was decent and didn't take it anyway when she changed her mind. But fuck, he'd had more of my girl than I've had, and it hurt. How the fuck did Trinity stand all those women I'd fucked? Seeing them when she'd come into the club, hear them talking about me? Seeing me go off or hang on them? God, I've been such a fool, trying to make her leave and move on, I'd only inflicted more and more pain on her. And, if it was even a fraction of how painful this was, this knowing that man had his head between her legs, her mouth on his dick, then I'd gutted her.

Chapter Eight

Trinity (Rapid City Clubhouse):

Walking up to the clubhouse doors, I tried to remember the name of the Prez of this charter was, but I would just tell them who I am and ask for the Prez. The compound where the Rapid City club was located was very different from our Vegas compound. Here there is no bar, no family complex, just one big ass warehouse that has a huge wall around it. From the outside of the warehouse, it just looked like an empty building. If it wasn't for the wall and electric fence with barb wire along the top you'd think the place was deserted. The only identifying factor was the RWMC emblem on the fence.

The doors opened and a tall dark-haired man came into the light of the overhead lamp outside the entry. He was larger than many, and husky, but his face was what drew my attention. He looked angry, flushed with it actually, and as he pushed past me he made some kind of negative comment about bitches looking for bikers, which with the lack of sleep and my overall attitude in general caused me to react, negatively.

"Hey, you fucker! Don't shove people out of the way." I shouted to the rude bastard that shoved me.

"Back off bitch, no parties tonight," he said, as he continued to move away from the door.

"Fuck off," I say, walking in the door.

The man turned and before I made it even a few steps into the clubhouse, he grabbed me by the hair, pulling me backward towards the door and tossing me out into the lot. I shouted and jumped up quickly, kicking out and hitting his knee, causing him to fall while reaching out to grab me. I stepped back, just as he was about to catch my hand.

"I told you bitch, no parties tonight, now get lost."

"Idiot, I'm no club whore! I am here from the Vegas Chapter, and, as soon as I call my Uncle Ranger, you will find out how fucking rude you really are." I said, stepping away from him even further.

"Christ, you must be kidding."

By now a few other brothers had come out to watch the show, but when I said that I was from Vegas, a couple of them started talking amongst themselves, then one of them went back inside, then came back a minute later with a tall thin man whose cut read President. Here was the man I was supposed to see when I arrived.

"What the hell Bear? You attacking women now?"

"Tried to tell her there were no parties tonight, she fucking went on in any way."

"Girl, that an RWMC cut on your back?" the president asked.

"Yes, I'm from Vegas, Ranger is my Uncle, I'm here for a few days. I'm on a personal run." I say to him.

"Bear, you get to call Ranger and explain how you assaulted his niece. Come on girl, let's get you settled. I'll call Vegas and let them know you are here safely."

73

"Thank you, Prez. I just need a room for a couple of days, then I'll be off again." I tell him.

"Let's grab a beer first girl, then you can tell me why you are running," he grinned down at me. "I know your daddy pretty good, and your Uncle Ranger and I served together. I know they'd never let their MC Princess on the road if they could have stopped you."

"I needed to find a new place to settle, so I agreed to use the charter clubs for stayovers, but I just want to see where I feel like stopping," I tell him.

"Only you left without giving them a chance to stop you huh?" he laughed.

"Well, yeah."

"You are your daddy's daughter!" he laughed. "I bet your mom is mad though, she never really liked the whole biker lifestyle, your dad just loves her more than anything, so he backed off a lot and tried to make her happy. Never understood that though he is the most loyal man I've ever met, and she just had trust issues."

"Yeah, sometimes I think dad misses being as involved as Uncle Ranger, but he goes on family or charity runs, and he goes to a lot of the parties. They both go to the family things, it's just the wild parties, dad goes home so mom isn't worried."

"Even after all these years?"

"Yes, I think dad is sweet for doing that for mom, but she shouldn't worry, my dad only has eyes for her."

"Well, I'm glad they are happy." He says, before walking me to the bar and grabbing a couple of beers from the beer cooler and grabbing up his cell phone.

I hear him talking to Ranger, as I pull out my phone, turn it on and call my dad.

"Hi, Dad!" I say.

"Trinity? Where the heck are you girl?" my dad sounds exasperated.

"In Rapid City, at the clubhouse."

"Good, you stay your ass put!" he tells me and I get a sinking feeling there is more.

"Why? Dad, I told you I'd check-in."

"Trinity, Joker is on his way to accompany you. I want you to wait for him, hear?"

"Dad, damn, I don't need anyone with me, especially Joker."

"Tough shit girl. I've been fine with you spreading your wings and all angel, but that shit you pulled in Laramie almost caused a decent man to be killed."

"What are you talking about?" I am really worried now, how could they know about Hoop?

75

"That man you took back to your motel Trinity, you didn't think anyone would know? You can't fuck with people's emotions like that girl."

"Dad, Hoop's emotions were not involved, nor were mine. And, I think who I decide to take back to my motel is my business, especially at my age!" I am so pissed I am about to hang up, get on my bike, and leave when his next words hit me like a physical blow.
"Maybe not Angel, but Pipes's emotions sure are engaged!"

"Pipes?" I ask, huskily. "Who told him?" I ask.

"No one had to, he overheard someone in the bar talking about you and Hoops, uh, hooking up. Man freaked out."

"Pipes is with Joker?" I ask.

"Yes."

"I gotta go, dad, I can't deal with this," I tell him.

I hang up, turn off my phone, then, thinking better of it I turn it back on and call Joker.

"Trinity?" He answers.

"Brother," I say
.

"What is going on, girl, where are you?"

"I'm in Rapid City, and according to dad you are on your way here," I say.

Pipe's Dream

"I am."

"Good, we are having it out when you get here and then I am leaving and you are NOT following me, got that?" I am so angry that I can barely even talk. The guys in the bar are watching me with speculative looks and some with lust. Oops, they like seeing me pissed, not a good time for this.

"See you soon baby sis." Was all he said before hanging up.

"Fuckin A" I say then turn back to the Prez who has a smile on his face.

"Your Uncle said to behave." He laughed.

"Where can I sleep?" I ask, giving in to the fact that this isn't going like I'd have wanted.

He calls over a prospect, Jerry something, and tells him to show me to an empty room, and then grabbing my beer, I follow Jerry something to a long hallway, to a room near the end of the hallway, and I thank him, and go into the room, closing the door, and settling down in just my bra and panties to sleep on a real mattress.

My sleep is disturbed a few hours later when my bedroom door is opened and then slams shut. I hear the lock engaging and briefly think to myself that I should have locked the damn door. Oh well, fucked that up.

"Who the fuck?" I say, turning to look at my intruder.

"Trinity, what do you think you are doing girl?" Pipes asks.

77

"Shit, couldn't you wait till morning to start with me?" I say. "It isn't like I haven't heard it all before anyway. Where is my brother?"

"He's in the bar."

"Ok, let me dress, we'll go out there to talk."

"No, you will talk to me now, here." He demands.

"Listen, Paul, I'm not feeling this right now, so don't push me," I say.

Pipes:

When she calls me by my given name, it cuts me. She only does that when she is dealing with extreme emotions. She is obviously upset, but I can't let this continue.

"Trinity, babe, I'm done with this. No more. I can't take it. Your father and the club, well they need to accept that you are mine or we'll leave the club, but I am NOT going on like this anymore. You are, and I am done, no more running, for either of us."

She sits up and looks at me, intently. "What are you saying?"

"I am telling you baby that I love you. I have tried to fight it for so long. But, no more. I can't deal with life without you."

"You sent me away after the party, told me you wouldn't be with me."

"I know, I'm so sorry baby, I was trying to stay away. But, when you left, I decided then that I couldn't do it anymore. I was letting you sleep off the drinking and I went over the next morning to talk, to tell you we'd go talk to your parents. But you were gone."

"I left that night. Having your last hope destroyed will sober you up pretty quick. How do I know this is real? How do I know that you are not just trying to get me home, then you are back to the club bitches and leaving me alone?"

"Because I am telling you that I love you and that I am never going to leave you again."

I walk over to her, I sit on the edge of her bed and I pull her onto my lap. Then, taking her face in my hands I look into her eyes. God, she is so beautiful, but her eyes hold a hurt, and damn, I put that hurt in her eyes. I am so sick about that. How in the fuck do I fix this?

"I know you know about Hoop, dad told me." She looks at me with worry now, wondering how I will react to this. I feel a rage but know it is my own fault so I try to tamp it down.

"Yeah, that fucked with me, I won't lie. But, it also made me realize how I've been hurting you with the whores. I am so damn sorry about that Trinity, I was only trying to make you hate me and move on, for your sake. I know now it was fucked up."

"Well, I am not sure how we'll deal with that when we go home, I can't take the club whores being with you, and I'm not going to be the kind of woman that ever shares."

"I'll never touch another woman but you, I swear, I only really wanted you anyway. They were poor substitutes for you."

"I won't be a forgiving kind of woman either, fuck one ever again and I won't come back to you." She is serious, I see it in her eyes.

"Never baby," and I am kissing her, slowly, like I am afraid she will disappear.

She pulls back and looks at me, "I didn't go all the way with Hoops, I couldn't do it."

"He told me, but he also told me what he did do, fucking killed me." I look into her eyes as I tell her this, and damn but she looks glad, good, let her get some justice if it helps, I deserve it.

"I am glad I didn't fuck him Paul, but I wish everything had been with you. I just gave up and figured I needed to move on. Hoops was kind. I would have been with him if I'd had time to get to know him better first. I just couldn't do it with a stranger. I planned to find someone in one of the charters to settle for, and not come home."

"I would have found you, babe, you have always been mine, I was too stubborn to admit it and fight for you, and you are worth the fight I just thought you deserved better than me."

"No, I deserve you, and you deserved me. Although, I have some trust issues with you now, so we have some things to work through."

"I know. Can we sleep for a bit? Let me just hold you?"

"Mmm Hmm, come on."

And she pulls the covers back, climbs into the bed and I follow her, pulling the cover over us both I wrap my arms around this incredible woman, that I've loved for my entire adult life, and I listen as her breathing slows, and she drifts off to sleep. It is a long time before I sleep, rather I just watch her sleep. Finally, her head is on a pillow next to my own. Thank Fuck!

I wake up the next morning and immediately I know she isn't in bed with me. Her side is cold to the touch. Fuck! If she took off I am going to tan her ass when I find her. I am up, dressed, and without even pissing I go running out of the room to look for my woman.

The relief I feel when I see her sitting at a table talking to Joker is so immense that I can barely contain it.

"Look, the sleepyhead is up," Joker says.
"Morning Pipes, you were sleeping so peacefully, I just let you sleep," Trinity says to me. Looking like she is apologizing for being gone. It goes a long way to defeating my anger and panic.

Scooting into the booth next to her I put my arm around the back of her shoulders, then pulling her to me I kiss her, I let her feel the panic and wanting, then I pull back.

"I did not like waking up and finding you gone," I tell her.

"I know, but I wanted to talk to my brother."

"I talked to Ranger this morning. He said that there are a couple of brothers here that want to patch over to Vegas, he wants us to meet with them and see if we think they'd be a good fit.

Then if so, bring them back with us for a trial period. Means we'll be here a few days before going back, but that could be restful." Joker tells me.

I can tell he isn't upset at the delay. He's been eyeing a couple of the women in the clubhouse and they've been eyeing him right back. Joker is a handsome man and the women are always flocking to him wherever he goes.

"He also said that there are some other ally clubs that have a couple of members wanting to move to Vegas, so I think we'll be adding to the ranks in the next few months." He adds.

"Well, I'm taking Trinity out for a bit so we can talk. You good here for a bit?" I ask him.

"Oh Yeah, I'm sure I can find something to occupy myself." He laughs, looking at one particular redhead that is giving him the same once over.

"I'm sure you will," Trinity says, standing up.

"Let's get dressed for the road, we'll take my bike," I tell her.

"I'll take mine too," she says.

"Nope, you are on mine today. I want to feel you on my bike woman, so no arguing." I tell her. She looked at me, then deciding to comply, she nods. Joker laughs.

"Better enjoy the wins when you get them, brother, my little sis is one hellcat! You need to be ready for the fights."

"Yeah, but the fire – it'll be worth it for the fire Joker," I say, following her to the room to get ready. We are going to sit down, have some food, and set some shit straight.

Trinity:

I can't imagine how we can get past some of the shit that has gone on between us. I used to think he was my best friend. Then, he took that from me, and Snake and Cat picked me up and helped me to be well through the loss of him. But over the years I've watched him with so many women, how can I get over that? I am nothing like those women, no matter how hard I try.

I have nice breasts, but nothing spectacular like all those club whores. My ass is a bit firm, but not rounded and sexy, I'm too athletic for that. And, I have some curves, but I'm tall and not round and shit I don't think I am ever going to be mistaken for a sex goddess. Not like Rory with her perfect body. I can dress hot, and I know I look good, my hair is my best feature and men seem to like it. But, even though I know I'm not bad, and actually, I'm pretty hot, I'm not sex kitten material. Nothing like the women I've seen him with over and over. How can an inexperienced girl like me keep a man that has so many beautiful women at his disposal?

I am afraid I'll open myself up to him and then he'll lose interest, then I know I won't survive the loss a second time, especially after I make love to him. I'd never be able to go home, never be able to see him at a club function with another woman. I'd die.

"Ready to go Trinity?"

"Yeah, where are we going?"

83

"There is a diner the club owns up the street a few miles. I thought we'd get some breakfast and talk. Then, if you'd like we can go for a ride and find a nice place to just sit and spend some time together."

"Ok," I tell him, but I dread this.

We pull into the diner lot and I see it is full of bikes. It is not just owned by the club, but frequented by the members. We ask for a secluded booth and when I sit down, Pipes waits for me to scoot and he sits next to me on the same side, shit. We order food, then he turns towards me, so I have to look into his eyes.

"Baby listen to me. I've told your dad I was coming after you. I told him why. I'm not going to go back to what was. I love you and I am not letting you go."

"I'm not sure we haven't gone too far away from each other Paul."

"It doesn't matter, we will fight our way back. I can't go on without you baby, I just can't."

"Well, see you forced me to have to accept a life without you. I've grieved for you, and I made up my mind to go, to leave my family, the MC family I grew up with, my home Paul. I had to accept that I couldn't be there anymore. It has been a hard decision and I don't know how to undo those feelings." I tell him. There is no reason to prevaricate, I need to just tell him. If we do have any hope of finding a way back, then I have to be honest.

"Ok, I get that. I will have to spend some time showing you that I am committed to you. I've hurt you and I get that. I'm so fucking sorry baby, please give me a chance to show you how sorry."

Then he leans over and kisses me. So sweet, so loving. I suddenly feel some hope, hope that we have a chance.

"Ok, I'm just going to come out and say it. I have watched you for years with all the sex kitten club whores. The sweet butts in the club and the hangers-on women have all been with you. Look at them, then me. I am inexperienced, I'm not a sex kitten, nor would I want to be one. How do I keep your interest? I can't go down this road and then lose you again. I'd not survive it." I tell him.

He takes his hand and reaches up, pushing my hair over my shoulder and cupping my face with his hand, then he tells me again that he loves me. And, that he will never leave me, never look at another woman, and that no woman could ever compete with me.

"Baby, those whores and club women are fake. They are just looking to get some biker dick, and they are hoping some biker will fall for them. They are shallow. I never sleep with them, I fucked them, yes. But they never spend the night with me, they don't talk with me, I don't share my world with them. It was sex, only sex. And often it wasn't even good sex, just a release."

"Well, just know this, I won't share. If you fuck another woman, regardless, I will leave, and you'll never find me again." I tell him.

"Not going to happen, baby. Not ever going to happen."

Pipes:

I take her for a ride, we ride for an hour, I hesitate to take her back to the clubhouse because I just love the feeling of her on my bike. When I finally do turn back, we decide to stop off for some items we need for the next few days. Then, after purchasing some toiletries, and snacks, and Trinity's favorite energy drinks, we go back to the clubhouse.

Joker is nowhere to be seen, so assuming that he is with some woman, I take Trinity up to our room and proceed to show her how much I love her.

Once we are in the room, I close the door and I pull her to me, kissing her and letting my passion for her show through the kiss as I pull her shirt off over her head.

"Christ baby, you are so beautiful," I tell her.

"I want you so bad, for so long Trinity, please baby, let me have you."

I am still kissing her but now I run my hands over her back, pulling her close and undoing her bra letting it slip down to the floor. Then I am kissing and licking her breasts. Running the pads of my thumbs over the erect nipples, my tongue playing with the nipple rings she has in her pierced nipples. She is so responsive, Those damn piercings are making her so sensitive.

And then I feel her pushing my cut off my arms and pulling my own shirt over my head. That woman, the one who complains about inexperience, leans over and kisses my nipples, and then she gently bites them.

"Oh fuck!" I say on a gasp. I've never had someone draw out a response from my nipples, damn.

Pipe's Dream

Then I undo her jeans, pushing them down and urging her to step out of them as I gently push her back towards the bed.

"No, take off your pants too, I want to see you, all of you. I've waited so long Paul." She tells me.

I take them off and then I am standing there in my black silk boxers and nothing else, she is standing in a red thong. We just look at each other, breathing heavily, our passions high, we just look.

"Paul, you are so handsome, I've always loved your body. I just, I never thought it would be mine."

"I know baby, I've always known you were mine, I just never thought I'd get to have you."

And then I just can't wait any longer. I push her to the bed, and when her legs hit the edge, she sits down and I kneel between her legs.

"Baby, I have to make you mine. I know that man had you, I have to erase that. I can't not do this, just relax baby. I promise you will not regret it."

"I want to touch you too."

"You will, but I need to purge this, then you can do whatever you want to me."

I know that isn't fair. She only had oral sex with that fucking Hoop, I'd had sex with many women. Blame it on the caveman mentality, I don't care, I only know I have to erase that man's claim on my woman.

I kiss her belly, and nip and lick my way down to her thong. Pulling it down, I just stare for a moment, pulling her lips open I stare at her.

"You have the most beautiful pussy I've ever seen. God baby, I have to have you."

"Paul?" she asks breathlessly. I know she wants me. But I need the words.

"What do you want baby? Tell me."

"I, I want, please, I want to cum."

"Ok baby, I can do that for you."

And then I bend down, and I kiss her, right on her center. I love the smell of her, I want the taste, I lick her I push my tongue into her and I am lapping at her soaking pussy, she starts moving, trying to push up against me and moving so much that I finally put my arm across her belly, holding her down and keeping her still while I lick and suck and kiss her. Then, I put two fingers into her and work her until I feel her about to climax, and then, biting gently down on her clit she screams out my name and cums so hard I feel her breathing stop.

"beautiful baby, so damn beautiful."

"Oh Paul, that was amazing. I want you to come inside me and make love to me fully."

Pipe's Dream

I look into her eyes, knowing that this was something that should have happened long ago, but at least it is finally happening now. I am so amazed that this woman loves me, wants me, and is giving me a chance to make things right for us.

I lay down beside her, pulling her up into my arms, then, kissing her and touching her, getting her excited again, I feel her tentatively reaching for me, she pushes her hand into my boxers and then pushing them down she releases my cock. I am so hard at this point that I can hardly stand it.

I watch in amazement as she leans over me and looks at me, she is pushing my boxers down further until they are far enough down that I can kick them off. Then she gets up on her knees, and settles over me, gazing like she hasn't ever seen a dick before.

"I didn't know you were pierced." She says.

"I knew your nipples were pierced, I knew when you did it too," I tell her.

"Oh yeah?"

"Yes, I was so pissed. If I could have figured out who that fucker was that pierced your nipples I'd have kicked his ass."

She snickered. Then, leaning down she licked my cock, just on the tip. Then she just takes me into her mouth and starts to suck and I know I am going to blow so I push her head away.
"No, not anymore baby. I need inside you, I don't want to cum in your mouth this time."

She just looks at me and so I push her back, then climbing between her legs I place myself near the entry of her opening, gently pressing into her, just a little bit. Holding myself back just long enough to ensure she was ready, rubbing my thumb along her clit, when she started to breathe heavier, I pushed into her completely.

"Oh my god, Paul."

"Are you ok baby?" I ask her.

"Oh yeah, I love you, Paul, I love you so much."

"Fuck baby, you feel so good," I tell her.

I've been with so many women, but damn, nothing has ever felt like this. Nothing and no one.

"Baby, I'm going to move now, tell me if I hurt you."

I began to push, in and out of her, slowly at first, then faster and harder. I feel her response to me, damn that woman is so responsive. I love the feel of being inside her.

"Oh baby, damn you are killing me."

"Paul, oh it feels so good."

"Baby, I don't know how much longer I can hold out, I need you to cum baby."

Paul, oh please." She is panting as I hold her, I lean over to kiss her. She starts to kiss me back, then as I feel her panting more and more, I move my face into her neck, kissing her along her collarbone. She follows suit and kisses me along my neck also, then as I feel her getting close to her climax, I increase my pace, getting closer and closer myself.

"Baby, I, oh god, I'm going to cum." She cries out.

"Yeah baby, oh fuck, cum baby." And I reach down and pinch her on her clit. And she comes apart, biting down on my shoulder, hard.

"FUCK! Yes, oh god." I feel my balls draw up and I cum, hard, and I keep driving myself deep inside her, drawing out my orgasm.

I lay there trying to catch my breath as I look at my woman, the love of my life, and can't seem to believe that this beautiful creature gave herself to me.

Rolling over, I pull her to me, close. And then kissing her face, her eyes, her mouth, I pull the sheet up and over us, then we sleep.

Chapter Nine

Trinity:

The noise woke me. It was so loud, reminding me that I wasn't used to living in the clubhouse. The temptation to go back to sleep was strong, but, I was hungry and sore. I needed a bath and food.

Going into the bathroom I noticed that it was a shower only, so, no bath. Oh well, I took a shower instead, letting the entire bathroom fill with steam from the hot water. Standing there with the water running down my body, I feel the tensions ease. Part of me can't believe it is real, Paul loves me, me Trinity, and he isn't denying it. I guess it just happened so quickly after so many years of struggle. I am just having a hard time accepting it.

Dressing after my shower, I notice that Pipes is still sleeping. So, knowing how clubs are, and since I am new here, I text Joker to see if he is out there, and surprise, surprise, he is. So, I ask for him to come to the hallway and escort me to some food!

I slip from the room, Joker is waiting and so he grabs me up and hugs me before leading me to the kitchen. I make a sandwich and sit at the table with my brother, talking.

"So, you and Pipes work it out?" he asks me.

"Yeah, but in truth, it just doesn't seem real, it's been so long that we've been fighting this, and just a week ago he was telling me it couldn't be, and now – here we are."

"You scared him sis, and then when he met Hoop, wow, that fucked with his head."

Pipe's Dream

"His fault," I say.

"He knows that too."

"Well, I'm happy, I guess I just have to give it some time, learn to trust that it's real and that he isn't going to wake up once we get home and decide it was a mistake." I am voicing my real fears now.

"It's not a mistake, the mistake was me being a dumb ass for the past couple years and trying to avoid the inevitable baby." Pipes says from where he walked up behind me.

He leans over and kisses me on top of my head before going to the counter to make a sandwich for himself.

"Well, I for one am glad you two finally have figured it out." My brother said.

"Wait a minute, you were always giving me ugly looks for even looking at her." Pipes says to Joker.

"Because brother, you needed to fight for her, not just sit back and let shit happen. And I'm sorry Pipes, but the groupies and bitches made me wonder if you would be faithful to any woman."

"This woman, this is the only woman I've wanted since she was seventeen. I've been drowning my sorrows with the others. I don't need that now that I have the real thing." He says, looking at me.

93

"Good, because now that you've claimed her, I'd kill you if I ever see you hurt her." And just like that, it's settled and we go on to finish our sandwiches.

"Well, since you are here now, take care of your woman, I'm going back to play with a sexy blonde that has decided I would make a good boy-toy for the night." Joker laughs as he gets up and ruffling my hair, walks out of the kitchen.

Chapter Ten

Pipes (one week later):

We pull into Vegas and pull over. Joker waves and goes on towards the clubhouse. We stop for a moment and Trinity stands with me beside my bike taking in the view of Las Vegas in the early morning light.

"We are home Trinity do you want to go anywhere first?"

"I'll call my parents, and we can go to the clubhouse later, can we just go to my apartment first?"

"Yeah, let's go there, but baby, I want us to start house hunting tomorrow, ok?"

"Isn't it too soon for that?" she asks.

"No, it isn't soon, we should have done this year's ago. I told you, baby, you are my forever, you and your delectable body are mine, we are getting a house that is ours, we are starting our life together, got it?"

"Got it."

It's nice to be home, even though I have some things still to work through with my woman. I just want to get to it. Home.

Trinity and I will stay here at her apartment until we can find a house, I don't want to live at her place, and she sure doesn't want to live at the clubhouse, so we are going house hunting right away. I told her we'd find a place to call our own. First, though, the big family night coming up. Her mom, dad, and Joker are expecting us for dinner.

"Trinity, hustle up babe, we need to run by the club so I can grab some clean clothes and still make it to your folks in time," I call out to her. She's been getting ready for this dinner now for two hours. What is she doing?

"Ready, let's go. I'm riding my bike." She tells me.

"Nope, not tonight babe, you are on my bike," I tell her.

"What's wrong with me riding?"

"Nothing, I just need you near, touching me," I tell her.

"Oh, well in that case, ok." She smiles at me.

"And stop looking at me like that or all that readiness you just went through will be for nothing," I tell her, grabbing her and holding her close.

"Let's go then, this is going to feel better when it's over." She tells me.

We ride to the clubhouse, and once we go in we see only a few brothers in the clubhouse, otherwise, it is rather quiet. I take Trinity's hand and we go upstairs to my room, where I toss her on my bed to wait while I dress. We are sitting there less than a minute or so when there is a knock at my door. I've already stripped down to dress, so I grab my clothes and head into the bathroom, leaving my woman to check who was at the door.

Pipe's Dream

I don't hear much as I start to dress, when suddenly the bathroom door bursts open and a very angry Trinity is standing there looking like she wants to kill someone, hell maybe me.

"Listen slick, I have been back in this clubhouse less than an hour and already your bitches are at the door looking for their favorite boy-toy. I told the slut you were off the market, but she doesn't believe me and wants you to bring your sexy self to the door, so she can, and this is in her words, welcome you home."

I finish slipping my shirt over my head, then kissing that angry mouth, I go to the door.

"You sure are sexy when you are pissed hellcat," I say, walking towards the closed door.

When I open it I see Connie, one of the Sweet Butts who I will say I've spent quite a bit of time waiting for me to open my door.
"Pipes!" She squeals, "you're home baby!" and then she throws her arms around my neck and starts kissing me before I can even stop her.

"Fuck!" I hear from behind me and know this is going very wrong.

"Cut it out Connie, I need to talk to you," I say.

"What Darlin, you miss me?"

"Connie, I have an Old Lady now. I finally got off my ass and claimed Trinity. You need to back off now."

"What? That princess is your Old Lady?" she asks.

Trinity just waves and gives a bit of her kind of advice.

"Yep, told you so you dumb slut, and I will give you a pass this one time for putting your hands on my man since you didn't know. But, no more. If you so much as brush up against him I will beat your ass and leave you on the damn street like all the other trash. So, pass the word, got it. I don't fucking share." Then, she walks up and moves me aside and slams the door right in Connie's face. Ok, then what a hellcat!

"Now, if you are ready," she says, "we can go talk to my parents about this situation." Then surprising me, she stands up on her toes and plants one on me, taking my breath away with that one move.

"Damn, I like pissed off jealous Trinity, that hellcat is sexy as shit baby. Let's be late?" I beg.

"Nope, just think about it. Then you can show me how you love me when we get home."

Walking out of the clubhouse a few minutes later, there are a number of women standing and watching as we head out. Connie is dead center of the group, and they are all glaring at Trinity. It is obvious that the word is out that I am off-limits. I decide to give Trinity a moment of triumph. I grab her up into my arms, her legs go immediately around my waist and I kiss her passionately, right in front of them all.

"What was that for?" she asks me breathlessly when we come up for air. I let her slide down my body, feeling my reaction to that kiss.

"Better than having you piss on me, don't you think?" I laugh.

"Yeah, probably." She laughs and runs out and heads for my bike.

Walking into her parent's house I felt like I did when I'd walked into the principal's office. Dinner was cooking, and the house smelt like pasta sauce and garlic, but when we walked into the living area, both her parents were sitting on the sofa, looking towards us with silent condemnation. Well, at least T-Man looked somewhat welcoming, but, her mother was completely cold and looked at me like she would like anyone but me to be standing in her living room.

"Hello, T-Man, Mrs. Flannagan," I say to them. "How are you both doing?"

"Hi Kids, come on in." T-Man said. Both of them stood and hugged Trinity who gave both of them kisses and hugs and then taking my hand she led me over to the love seat. We sat down and continuing to hold Trinity's hand, I looked at T-Man and decided it was best to just speak up and get it over with.

"I want you to know that Trinity and I are together now, I am not going to fight this any longer. I love her, and she loves me." I say to them.

"Are you just keeping her as an Old Lady or are you forever? Marrying her and being monogamous?" Her mother asked.

"Mom don't," Trinity said.

"No, Trin, she has the right to ask," I say.

"I love her, and we are barely into this. I want her to be my old lady, my wife, the mother of my children, and the woman I grow old with. But, we will do all that on our timeline. We need to take this in steps, so we can find our way. But don't worry about monogamy, Trinity is it for me, I don't want or need anyone else, she is mine and I am hers." I tell her.

I must have said something right, she nodded at me and stood, before looking at us again and walking towards the kitchen.
"I'm Jennifer, by the way." She threw over her shoulder at me as she walked to the kitchen. Both Trinity and T-Man smiled at me. I guess I was accepted.

Joker came in soon after and we had a nice family dinner. Joker had already come to terms with us being together during our time in Grand Rapids. So, our dinner conversation was pleasant until the topic of the party this weekend at the clubhouse came up.

"Party is family only until nine then it will be party central," Joker said.

"Sounds like fun, do they expect us to play too?" I ask.

"Nope, not this time. You two can enjoy the party yourselves."

"Well, we have to start back up at Rage next weekend, so it is good to have this weekend off," I say.

"Trinity, don't you work at Rage with Cat next weekend?" Joker asks her.

"I don't know anymore. I was supposed to, but when I left I think Snake may have made other arrangements. I do know that Rory isn't working much right now, and Cat is just back. The guys are supposed to work Wednesdays for the Ladies night, but I don't think that they are available too much on the weekends," Trinity says.

"You should call Snake and let him know you are home," I say.

"I will, but we'll probably see him at the party anyway and I have to go see Lissey, I've missed two weeks of Monday adventures with her. I need to let her know I'm here," she says.

Shortly afterward, Trinity begged off with the excuse of being tired, so we left to head home. I noticed that she was upset and quiet when we got home, and I needed to find out what was going on and clear this shit up quick. I know this woman and she will go off in her head and get all kinds of screwed up.

Trinity:

Shit, this was something I didn't think about. Parties mean whores, whores who have been with Pipes a lot more than me, and the damn band, groupies. Why am I so damn insecure? Me? I am a fucking hot ass woman! I can't be like this, I don't want to be that woman. But shit.

"Trinity, what is wrong? Baby, I know you've gone somewhere in that head of yours. Talk to me." Pipes tells me, as he lifts my chin so he can look into my eyes. No hiding there.

"It's nothing. I'm just being silly, don't stress it." I tell him. I'm hoping he will just let it go. Of course, one can hope, doesn't mean much in the scheme of things.

101

"Trinity, tell me." He insists. I know I am not getting out of this.

"Paul, I just realized I'm going to have to get my jealousy under control. Parties at the club will not be easy at first. Maybe after a bit, and I don't want to be my mother, all paranoid and causing you to be uncomfortable with the club. I've watched my dad, he misses the brotherhood. He doesn't often come to the parties because they upset my mother. I LIKE to party, I just don't want to fight my way through them."

"Baby don't worry. Me and this bod belong to you and only you. You are borrowing trouble. As far as fighting, don't bother. I do know how to say no, what about you?"
"What do you mean?"

"Guys are always wanting to dance with you too, when I am on stage and you want to dance, am I going to have to look at you dancing with other men?"

"No, I'll dance alone or with the girls. I don't want other hands on me."

"Ok, so we understand each other then?"

"Yes."

"Good, now let's get on to something much better than worrying about something that isn't going to be a problem."

Then he picks me up and runs towards the bedroom. I find myself tossed on the bed on my back, looking up at my man, yes, my man in all his beautiful manly form, looking down at me with intense hot eyes. He's mine, M-I-N-E, no club bitch can touch him! If they do, I'll go all Freddy Kruger on them.

I want this man in every way.

"Baby?" I ask as he starts to unhook his pants.

"Hmm?" He says, then his pants are being pulled down, and I stare.

"Damn, is that all for me?" I ask, looking at his very hard erect cock, it seems to jump out of his boxers as he pushes them down.

"You my woman?" he asks.

"You my man?" I ask him back.

"Yes, baby."

"And I am yours," I say to him. His cock is so beautiful, all hard and soft at the same time. His piercing makes it look badass, like all the ink on his body does. I watch as it jumps as I continue to look at it and licking my lips I think about taking it in my mouth.

"Baby, you are making me very hungry with the way you are eye fucking my cock! Get those pants off, now woman."

I slide my pants off but I don't take off my panties, then he leans over me and pulls my shirt off over my head, then without hesitation, the bra follows.

I spread myself, just enough to draw his gaze to my center and his eyes get darker, hotter if that is possible.

"God woman, see how slick you are for me? Even with those little panties on I can see how wet you are. I do believe my woman needs her man's cock."

"Take me, Paul, take me now."

"I will, right now,"

And then he reaches down and pulls the panties off me. "On all fours, now!" he demands.

Expecting to find him at my hips, pulling me into him I get balanced, and then looking behind me I see him laying on his back, sliding up between my legs.

"Fuck my face baby, I want to taste how much you want me."

"Oh hell." My body shutters, but he doesn't wait for me to settle, he grabs me and pulls me down onto his face and I don't have time to fuck his face because he is fucking me with his mouth, his tongue, and I can't take it. It is too much.

I want him in my mouth too, I try to get him to let me turn around, so I can suck him at the same time. He is turning his head back and forth in a NO motion, all the while nipping at my clit and causing me to pant all the harder. I try to move off him, wanting to turn around and taste him too, but he grabs onto my ass, harder, pulling me into him so hard I am impaling myself on his tongue.

I am so close, I start rubbing up and down on him and then I go over, crying out his name and trying to wrench myself out of his hands as I become so sensitive I can hardly take it. After he laps at me for a minute, he slaps my ass and lets me climb off him.

I lay next to him and he kisses me with all the passion he is feeling, letting me taste myself on him. I wouldn't have thought this would be hot, but knowing he is covered in my taste, he was down there, loving me with his mouth, and knowing I turned him on, well it's hot as fuck!

"Baby, I love that you don't mind a taste of yourself on my face and my tongue, makes me crazy woman, he groans into my mouth.

I let my hands roam, not breaking our kiss I just pull at him until I feel him pressing down on my breasts. Then, he is kissing my breasts, nipping and licking my nipples, flicking at the nipple rings, until I think I may cum just from his mouth on my breasts.

"God, I love you, your subtle skin, your responsive nipples, your delicate folds that are sweet as fuck, Christ," he breaths out, then he is again touching me, teasing me.

I'm done with teasing, I want him. I push him down, onto his back and then smiling down at him I climb onto him, straddling him and reaching behind me I grasp his cock and lifting up I guide him into me. Going slowly for a minute, watching his face as I take control and then I slam down on him, hard and fast.

His head jerks up and he grabs my ass and lifts me up and then he slams me back down. Then, after only a couple strokes, he flips me over and pulling my legs up over his shoulders, he slams back into me, hard and fast, owning me, in full control of my body.

"Aww god, woman, you feel so damn good."

I am crooning, not even able to form words, It feels so good, he is filling me, his piercing is rubbing my g-spot each time he enters me and when he pulls out, with that twist of his hips I feel like I am being shocked, the pleasure is so intense.

"Paul, aww baby, I'm so close."

I feel the heat building, it is almost too much, I am on fire, and I can't even keep my eyes open I am so far from having any control over my body. I scream out my release, then he pulls out, and while staring into my eyes, he gives his cock a couple more strokes and cums all over my stomach, my breasts, and the look in his eyes as he marks me with his cum - hot enough that I feel myself building up again.

Paul seems to sense that I am responding to his claiming, marking me with his seed, and reaches to me and pushes two of his fingers deep into me, curving his fingers to hit that spot that is sure to send me over. The heat of the encounter is so strong that it fires my passion once again and it only takes a couple more strokes for me to cum on his hand.

Smiling at me, he pulls his fingers from my pussy and sticks his fingers in his mouth, smiling as he licks them clean.

"Fucking beautiful," he says. "Know this, now and forever, you are mine, baby. Mine."

Then, he lifts me, carries me to the shower, and after getting the water adjusted, he lifts me into the shower and cleans me, before drying me and holding me all night while I sleep.

Chapter Eleven

Trinity:

I woke the next morning and realizing we were low on groceries, left Pipes sleeping as I dressed quietly, and went out to pick up some breakfast until I could buy food later in the day. I was back quickly with coffee bagels and cream cheese when I heard the shower running in the bathroom.

Ahh, my man was up and showering. Taking a coffee for him and mine I walked to the bathroom. The door was open, and I could see through the glass door that he was not just washing, but he was stroking himself.

My breath caught in my throat, god that was hot. As if he senses me, he groans through clenched teeth and turns to see me watching him. He stops for a moment, then staring at me he again begins to stroke himself.

"I love seeing your hungry gaze on me while I'm pumping my cock." He says in a groan.

He steps closer to me, as he continues to handle himself. I can't say anything; my own breathing becomes labored. I want him so bad, I want to taste him. But, just as I am trying to move, make myself go to him, he starts to cum, shooting onto the tile as he groans out his release. I am mesmerized, I just stare, until the last drop has finished, and he cleans himself up.

He steps out of the shower, grabs me, and pulls me to him, and kisses me.

"Good Morning baby." He says.

"Yeah, I bought bagels, but now I think that I should have stayed here."

He laughs at me and then pulls me to the bedroom where he shows me I didn't miss a thing while our coffee gets impossibly cold.

Pipes:

I'd only just finished loving my woman when my phone rang. Cursing I pulled it up and looked at it. Seeing it was Doc, I answered.

"Yeah?"

"Church, asap." Was all he said. Then, without any other info, he hung up.

"Shit! Baby, I have to go, club business." I tell her. She moans but rolls off me to let me up.

"I'll let you go, Uncle Ranger must need you. But, don't be any longer than you need to, I'm cooking for us tonight and I'm inviting Snake and Rory.

"Love you, baby."

"Love you too, now get to it."

I could sense the feeling of unease in the clubhouse when I walked in. Something was going on. Dropping my phone with the others in the tub on the table outside the chapel, I walked in and took a seat, getting slaps on the back by my brothers that know I've just got back from finding and claiming Trinity.

"Ok, we have a couple of items of business that need discussing today," Ranger says.

"First, welcome back Joker and Pipes, glad you found Trinity and brought her home. Pipes, can we all assume you've claimed her?" he asks me.

"Yes sir, she's mine," I say. To hoots and foot-stomping by my brothers.

"Good, it's about time." He tells me.

"Now, we have several brothers from other charters wanting to patch in and a couple from other clubs that are allies that want to come over to RWMC. Three came back with Joker and Pipes from Grand Rapids, they vouch that they are good men, so we will meet them at the party tomorrow night, and then we'll vote on Saturday about them. There are two from Georgia, the Columbus charter, and one from the Baton Rouge charter. Then we have three Falcons that want to patch over to RWMC, they are moving to Vegas and since we are allies with the Falcons, and there isn't a Falcon charter around here, we are offering them a full patch over if they are approved and voted in."

"Are they all here this weekend?" Fox asks.

"Yes, they are all coming in today and tomorrow, the party is going to give us a chance to meet them. Make a point brothers of getting to know them, that way you will be able to vote. They are all invited to the barbeque, then the party. We need them to see that we are very family oriented here, it's not just Sin City." Ranger finishes on that subject.

"Now, Doc, give us the intel on our problem."

"Ok, brothers, Big John is gone from San Diego. No one knows if he was voted out, if he just left or if he's dead. He is just gone. Viper has taken over as the President and the club has taken a new direction. It looks like they are recruiting like mad, taking anyone with a record, that swears loyalty to Viper. He is very verbal that they are going to take over the gun pipelines and bring the money back into San Diego. He also has sworn a vendetta against all RWMC charters, not just Vegas. His promise to his recruits is that he'll take our money and our most prized possessions and make us pay."

"What the fuck does that mean?" Rayne asks.

"I want everyone to be on alert for anything that looks out of place. It could mean nothing, or it could mean he is going to go after our families. Not sure yet. I am sending Geek and a couple of brothers to plant some cameras and listening devices at their clubhouse, and to tap their phones. But, as you know most real info is passed on via burner phones. So, listening devices at the clubhouse will be our best bet."

"Why don't we take a sweet butt with us to go inside. She could plant some bugs around." Ruger asks.

"We could ask one of them, but if they are pissed at us, it could backfire," Doc says.

"I'll get one for you," Joker laughs, "promise she won't be anything but happy."

That gets a lot of laughs and Joker got the assignment, find a sweet butt to do us this solid. We'll also be paying her a ton of cash for her efforts.

"Brother don't ask Connie," I tell him. "Your sister went all hellcat on her yesterday."

"Damn, that girl is a spitfire." He laughs.

"Pipes, you are going to have your hands full the next few weeks after all your exploits," Ranger tells me.

"I didn't raise no girly girl, she will kick some ass if you get out of line," T-Man adds.

"Yeah, I've been warned," I say, amid laughter and catcalls of pussy whipped ring out. And yeah, I guess I am.

"Brothers," I say. "If a man has to be pussy whipped, well that's the woman to do it," I say, not wanting to get too graphic with her dad, uncle, and brother in the room.

I go back out to the offices. Before I left to find her I ordered her a cut, with Property of Pipes on it and I was going to see if it came in. I want her to wear my property label before we go to the party. I don't want anyone, especially any new members, hitting on her.

Josie is sitting in the office, sorting some paperwork for Ranger when I go in.

"Hi, Josie!" I say, thrilled to see her, my surrogate mom. I am hugging her and laughing at her obvious happiness at seeing me.

"I bet I know why you are here!" she says, reaching for a box with my name on it.

"Good, it came in," I say, opening the box and looking at it. Smiling I am so excited to go home and show it to her.

"Where are you staying? At her apartment?" Josie asks.

"For now, we are talking to a realtor today about houses. I want to buy a house, for us, so it isn't hers or mine."

"Good idea," Josie says. "It will be good for her to know you are serious, she's spent a long time waiting for you."

"Damn, Josie. I was trying to leave her alone, let her have a different life as Jennifer wanted for her." I say.

"Understood, but some things are just meant to be. And Paul, honey, I can tell you from my own experience that the MC lifestyle can be wonderful and rewarding if you are secure in your marriage. Ranger and I have never had problems being married and in the MC. Jennifer just had a bad experience and couldn't get past it. I took control of the bitches coming on to my man early on, and they learned to leave him alone. Sometimes a new bitch comes into the club and thinks she can get with the President. Ranger tells her no, then he tells me. I know he will always tell me when a woman is coming on to him so I can handle it, woman to woman. Just like you men want to handle the men that come onto your women. Just never hide or keep it from her and she will trust you. And, make her know you also expect her to never keep it from you when a man comes on to her. You trust each other to handle the shit, and you will be fine."

"That is good advice Josie, thank you. I'll talk to her and that will keep us from misunderstandings, I hope."

"Well, it's a place to start. Now go home and see your girl, she needs to have that cut for the party tomorrow night."

Trinity:

We spend the morning looking at houses the realtor called us about. None of the ones we looked at grabbed us and made us think home. So, we keep on looking. We've agreed that we want a house that is one story, has at least three bedrooms, an office or den, and a pool. I would like enough land that I cannot hear my neighbors fart from their bathrooms, but that is hard to get in Vegas. We've decided to look further out of town, maybe even beyond Blue Diamond, so we can have some land too.

I am looking forward to seeing all my crew tonight at the party. Our Angel Crew is growing! It used to be me, Penny and Cat. Now we've added Rory, and Caro likes to hang with us too. She's a bit young but you wouldn't know it by her actions. You can tell most of her teen years were spent with three brothers raising her. There are other old ladies, but they are older and more mom and Josie's age, they are not crazy and wild like we are. Plus, for the most part, they are not fighting off the bitches like we have to. Our men are too recently claimed. The sweet butts and club bitches don't like losing regular dicks to an old lady, so we Warrior Angels have to stick together.

We go early to the clubhouse, I am wearing my tight skinny jeans with knee-high boots and a white tank under my cut. I have a Property of Pipes cut on! He means to claim me for real, in front of the entire club! I am ready to go to Sinner and get inked! Pipes says we are going tomorrow afternoon. I am still trying to decide

113

where to get the ink placed and how to design it. Cat has an idea and we are going to try to draw it up tonight. I don't want Pipes to see it, I want to surprise him. We'll see.

Walking into the family area, I notice a lot of new faces. Pipes told me that there were a lot of new members being considered for a patch over from other charters. I was excited to hear Fletch and Raven are coming down from Reno. Raven is so much fun, the couple times we met in Reno when Dad took us up there we got on great. Her brother is transferring down to Vegas with his job and is patching into our chapter. Fletch and Joker became good friends too so that is nice.

Seeing my crew, I kiss Pipes and walk over to the girls.

"Hey there chickie, let's see that cut." Cat calls out to me.

I turn around, spinning and laughing and showing the cut to my crew. Cat has her cut on and so does Rory. Caro looks at us and laughs and calls us boring old ladies. Penny agrees, she isn't ready to settle down either.

"Hey Penny, remember Raven, Fletch's sister?" I ask.

"Aren't they from Reno?" she asked.

"Yeah, they are coming here. They should be here today."

"Another angel to join our crew," Cat says.

"She's our age, Cat, so she may be attached, or looking for an attachment."

"Well, we have plenty to choose from, maybe she will piss off the sweet butts too." We all laugh at that.

Fox walked over and came up behind Cat, lifting her off the bench, he carries her away laughing telling her it was time to eat. Those two had a hard time when Cat was abducted. Now she is ready to pop out a baby and Fox doesn't miss a chance to pamper her. Rory is a few months pregnant too and we are all excited to see what she is having. She didn't want to know so none of us know.

A commotion burst out and I saw Joker and Fox shouting and high-fiving a brother and then Raven ran from behind him and straight to us.

"Raven!" I shout. "Welcome to Vegas."

"Hey, good to be here. I sure needed a change, I was so happy when Fletch decided to move, and bring me with him."

"We're sure glad to have you girl, are you ready for the party tonight?" Rory asked.

"Yep, but doesn't look like you get to party, preggers huh?"

"four months now," Rory answered.

"Cat is due anytime now," I tell her.

"Cool, lots of babies."

Pipes:

Trinity seems to be having a lot of fun with the girls. Her "crew" is growing now with the addition of Raven, and with Caro spending more time with the women, I hope those gals don't rub off on my baby sis. Most of the kiddos have gone home or been put down in the family rooms. The music is kicking up and the party is getting geared up. I'm going to find my woman and keep her close during the party. Too many new faces and I don't want any trouble tonight. Too many times I'll be playing during parties, I want to spend the time I'm not singing with my girl.

She is right in the middle of all the women, as usual. People do tend to gravitate to Trinity, she is quite the attention gatherer. I walk up behind her, putting my arms around her waist and pulling her back against me.

"Baby let's go dance. I want your attention tonight, too many nights I'll be singing and not able to dance with you. Tonight is all mine, ladies so tell her bye." I tell the Angels.
"Bye girl have fun!" Raven tells her.

"I want to dance all night!" Trinity says on a laugh.

I pull her out of the group of women and half carry her to the bar where the music is playing.

"This isn't as good as you singing, I love your voice!" Trinity tells me.

"I'll sing for you anytime, baby."

I nuzzle into her neck, kissing her and holding her. Then we are dancing and the music is nice, but I start singing to her while we are singing. I know I have to meet these new guys

116

through the night, but not yet. For now, I just want to hold my woman and dance.

The night is perfect. All my brothers are congratulating us, telling me I'm so lucky to have the Princess all to myself. And they'd be right. Trinity has been the MC Princess her entire life. Along with Penny, these two girls are the most sought after, and most off-limits women in the MC.

We take a break and go over to the bar to get a drink when I see a familiar face that makes my stomach drop and my rage explode; Hoop is standing in our bar! I make our way to the other side of the bar and am seriously thinking about taking her to my room to make love when Joker comes up and asks me to step aside a minute. I already know where this is going and want Trinity to never see this fucker.

"Pipes, need to speak to you brother." Joker calls out.

"Trinity, go chat with Cat, she is sitting and looking lonely since she is about to pop. I'll be over in a sec baby." I tell her.

"Sure, she does look tired huh?"

As she makes her way to Cat, I go over to Joker.

"Did you see him?" he asks me.

"I did, what is he doing here?"

"Not sure, heard Ranger say that some Falcon MC members were wanting to patch over, he may be one of them."

"Fuck no, I will not have him here," I say.

117

"Dude, that is B.S. Do you see all these club whores?

You've had most of them if not all of them. Trinity has to see all of them. You are screwed up over one man that didn't even screw her. I think you need to get over it."

"Not fair man, I don't expect her to see the club whores on a daily basis, but I'd have to be brothers with this man."

"You do know that is not true right? She sees these chicks every time she is at the clubhouse."

"Fuck, I don't know if I can do this without losing my shit Joker."

"Well you need to get ready, he spotted you and he's looking around, probably looking for Trinity."

I see him, and I see Trinity with Cat, I go over to her without a backward glance. Picking her up, I sit in her seat pulling her onto my lap.

"Baby, one of the men here to see about patching into our chapter, Uhm, one of them we know." I don't know how to tell her.

"Oh yeah? Who is it?" She is looking at my face and cuddling close to me.

"Hoop." I just say it. And I am watching her face to see how she takes it.

118

"Hoop?"

"Yeah, and don't look now but he is coming over to us." I tighten my arms around her.

"Hi there Angel, what are you doing in Vegas? Last I knew, you were going to Grand Rapids."

"Hi Hoop, I live here, this is my home."

"Well, small world. I see you found her there Pipes wasn't it?" he asks me.

"Yes, I found her."

"Well, good. You happy now Angel?" he asks my woman.

"I am Hoop, thanks." She seems to genuinely like this asshole.

"Well, save me a dance Angel, looks like I am going to like Vegas!" and then he walks away.

"You are NOT dancing with him," I tell her. She just laughs and shakes her head no. She knows better than to have anything to do with Hoop.

Joker comes over then, smiling, and asking his sister to dance. Of course, I let her go dancing with him, and it was then that things got interesting.

Trinity:

119

Raven Featherwood

Hoop being here was a surprise, but not a bad thing. It isn't his fault that I singled him out in Laramie to be a stand-in for Pipes in the bedroom. He knows the score and so does Pipes. But Joker wants to give me a lecture.

"Trinity, you ok with Hoops?" he asks me.

"Yeah, I'd rather no one else is told about what happened. But I am not too disturbed. I can handle it if Pipes can."

"Well, steer clear of him and Pipes should be ok."

I'm dancing with my brother, and thinking about the odds of Hoops showing up in Vegas, when I look over to my man to see three, yes three club whores walking up behind him. He doesn't see them coming because he is talking to Cat, but she does and before she can say anything all three of them wrap around him, one plopping her ass on his lap.

He does look shocked and starts trying to disentangle himself from them but not before the one on his lap wraps her arms around his neck, and pressing her tits into his chest she plants one on him.

"No, she fucking didn't!" I say, disentangling myself from Joker and heading to Pipes.

I must say that rational thought had left me. Poor Cat, so pregnant couldn't do anything, and Fox had gone to check on Lissey who was sleeping in the family section so she didn't even have any backup from him.

Before Pipes can even push the bitch off his lap the other two see me coming and looking at me like they got on over on me,

120

they just stand there smirking at me. The dumb bitch on his lap doesn't see me coming though and I grab her by the hair and yank her skanky ass off my man.

"Bitch! Do you have a death wish?" I say to her as her ass hits the floor.

"Fuck, you stupid skank, what the fuck are you doing? I was just kissing him hello."

"You fucking keep your hands off. I know you know he is now taken. Connie fucking told you already. You are just trying to push my buttons. Too fucking stupid!" I say to her then grabbing her up by her hair, once she stands up I drag her through the crowd, much to the amusement of many of the brothers.

"Get her hellcat!" Gunner yells out to me.

"Damn, brother your woman is a badass!" Styx calls out to Pipes.

I don't care, I am pissed this stupid bitch thinks she can fuck with my man. I drag her kicking and screaming right to the front door where I plant my foot in her backside and push her out the door.

"Don't fucking come back either whore!" I shout.

I look around and see Uncle Ranger laughing, and I know that I didn't just fuck up and overstep. I walk right up to him and kissing him on the cheek, tell him that I'll leave the rest of the club whores alone if they leave Pipes alone.

"Hear that everyone?" Ranger shouts out. "Princess here agrees to leave the rest of the women alone as long as they leave Pipes alone. I suggest you listen, the Flannagan Princesses are hellcats!"

This brings about a lot of shouts, foot stomps and I don't even make it halfway back into the room before Pipes grabs me up and throws me over his shoulder and takes off down the hallway and up to his room.

"Come on Hellcat, that was sexy as shit, need to tame you down a bit though." He says to me amid a lot of laughter and catcalls. Well shit. I think we both just won that round!

Chapter Twelve

Trinity:

We are back at Rage and I LOVE this place. I don't go upstairs, I just love the bar, the dancing, and tonight my man is playing and I can't wait. I love his voice and he is so hot up on stage, and now instead of being jealous – I know whose bed he will be in tonight! Mine!

I just finished a bar dance with Snake and now we are getting ready for Pipes band to play. I'm told to take a break and go to the VIP area during the first set. This will be our first time since we've been together that he is on stage.

Snake hands me a drink and some waters for the band, and I head over to the VIP stand. It is funny, not that I'd have ever thought I'd laugh about this, but the woman talking about the band members is kind of funny tonight. The joke is on them. They can talk about Pipes all they want, that man is MINE.

I sit down after putting the waters on the stage where the guys and Caro can get them easily, then I just wait and listen.

"Girl this band is hot, I've heard them several times." A blonde bimbo says to her friends.

"I heard that if you get right up front you can hook up with the band after they play," another says.

"Yeah, they are all hot ass bikers too, double the badass," still another says.

"I did the drummer once, that man is too sexy," the first blonds says.

"Well I want to do the lead singer, I am going to flash him my tits tonight. I hear he is too hot and that his dick is huge and pierced!" a redhead says.

"Well, good luck, I have a friend that goes to the MC clubhouse for parties and he has an old lady now, and she is a bitch, kicked a girl out last week for kissing him."

"Oh well, what she doesn't know doesn't hurt," the redhead says.

I of course say nothing. I just sit back, drink my drink, and listen. I will kill a bitch if she touches him. She can flash her tits all she wants, Rayne, Winter, or Styx may like her rack, but if any bitch touches Pipes, well, that's on her.

The lights start to flash and the band comes out with a lot of fanfare, it's been a while since they've played. Pipes is looking around and I realize he is looking for me when he sees me and smiles. The women standing in front are screaming at the band and trying to get their attention. Pipes doesn't even look at them, he has eyes only for me.

"Hello everyone! Good to be back at our favorite venue; Rage!" he shouts.

"Before we get started, I have a special song I want to sing to a special woman. Trinity, baby come here." The band starts a drumroll, and I get up and walk around to the steps and go up to him.

124

"I've been blessed recently to have this amazing hellcat agree to love me forever. So, baby, I have a special song to sing to you." Then he turns to his band, his brothers and sister, and nodding his head they start to play *Marry Me by Train.*

I stand there, tears in my eyes, while he sings his proposal to me, in front of the entire bar, he even gets down on his knee in front of all these people and pulls out a ring box and opening it he pulls out a beautiful diamond ring and places it on my finger, right up on stage.

Then as the song ends he wraps me in his arms and lays one on me. I hear shouting and cheering and realize my parents are there, much of the MC family is there and Snake is on the bar shouting at me, Cat is sitting in the VIP section with Fox, clapping and smiling. I kiss him again and taking the microphone from him, look at the bitches in the front of the stage, and in parting give my own little speech.

"Ladies, this sexy band up here loves attention, but this man right here," I point to Pipes, "taken. So, save yourselves a beat down, hands off!" Then laughing, I blow him another kiss and walk off stage, straight to my friends in the VIP area. Holding my ring finger up, proudly showing off my engagement ring.

Cat hugs me close, telling me that was the most romantic proposal she's ever seen or heard of. Fox's proposal to her was pretty hot too, but yeah, I think my man wins!

I will show him how much I loved his proposal later when we go home. Oh yeah, he will definitely get a thank you.

We are sitting and listening to the band, and Pipes keeps looking at me and smiling. Those women that were talking about him earlier keep looking at me too and I have to admit, it feels good knowing that they are looking at me and wishing they were me. So many times I used to look at the groupies and wish I was them. Now, it was worth the pain and the heartache, I get the happily ever after, only me.

Suddenly, over the sound of the music and despite my total occupation with watching my man perform, I hear Cat give out a groan, and looking to see what is wrong, I see her face pinched into a painful-looking scowl. Oh shit, the baby!

"Cat, are you in labor?" I ask her in a panic.

"Oh Trinity, it hurts, I think it's time." She says.

"I'll find Fox, I think he is at the bar, hang on honey."

I go running off looking for Fox, seeing Snake, I send him to get her while I try to find Fox. I don't immediately see him, but the band sees the activity and Pipes stops singing the song that they are singing and calls out over the microphone.

"Cat, is it time?" and she lets out a cry right about that time, and with the music stopped and everyone stopping to see what is going on, her cry is heard throughout the place. Fox of course hears and comes flying towards his wife, just as Snake picks her up and starts to carry her to the door.

"Trinity, baby I'll meet you there as soon as we finish!" Pipes shouts out over the microphone. I wave to him and follow Snake and Fox out of Rage and to the SUV that Fox drove tonight.

"Fox, hurry, it hurts." She is struggling now.

"Be there soon kitty cat, just hang on," Fox tells her.

126

Pipe's Dream

I am riding in the back seat with her. Holding her hand, while Snake is upfront with Fox. He is calling the clubhouse, telling the brothers, and he's called Ranger already so now we are just trying to get to the birthing center as quickly as we can.

"Here we are, Darlin." Snake tells her.

It was agreed that in addition to Fox, Snake and I would be with her during delivery, we are her best friends and the godparents to the baby, so we have to be there. Fox only agreed to Snake as long as he stays by her head. He is not allowing another man to see her below the waist, even during childbirth.

Snake of course is fine with that, he has no desire to see that anyway. Rory was laughing and told him to prepare because he was cutting the cord when their baby comes in a few months. He is about to get an education. Rory didn't want to be in the delivery room, she thinks ignorance is bliss. She'll have to go through this soon enough and would rather not stress any sooner than she has to.

The nurse attaches the fetal monitor to her, gets her in a gown, and all set up for the delivery when they check her, and all of a sudden there is a lot of activity.

"Cat, your baby is ready to come out. No waiting, next contraction you can push."

"Doesn't labor last hours?" I ask the nurse.

"Usually, but after the first, it can happen quickly." The nurse replies.

Then the doctor is again telling her to push, and damn if that girl doesn't just grab my hand, Snakes hand, and Fox is behind the head of the bed holding her up and she pushes and lets out one hard groan and then the most beautiful sound I've ever heard; the cry of her baby boy!

"Oh my god, Fox, he's here, he's finally here." She is crying, but they are tears of joy.

Fox is kissing her, crying himself and they bring the baby and lay him on her belly and let them see him for a minute before taking him to clean him up while she delivers the afterbirth and gets herself cleaned up and stitched.

"What is his name mom and dad?" the nurse asks.

"Jack Thomas Flannagan," Cat tells the nurse. "Jack after his great-granddad, and Thomas after my dad. J.T. for short," then again, Fox is kissing her.

"Listen you two, J.T. is amazing. We are going to go out and give you all some privacy. Can we tell them out there or should we wait for you to announce?" I ask.

"Go ahead you two, you are her besties, and you are the godparents, you announce. I just want to hold my woman for a bit, I missed this last time with Lissey." Fox says, never taking his eyes off his wife.

Come on Snake, let's go tell the masses that there is a new Road Warrior to patch in.

Then when we walk out to the family waiting area, the waiting area is full, the hallways are full and the nursing staff is overwhelmed by all the scary alpha males in the hospital OB waiting area. All of them are claiming to either be grandparents, or uncles and aunts, which of course he nurses don't believe for a minute, but not one of them will challenge the men.

Snake is holding my hand until we get out and Rory comes up to her man and Pipes comes up to me. Taking me in his arms he asks how she is. I turn to Snake and tell him to tell everyone.

"Trinity and I are godparents to the most amazing little boy, Jack Thomas Flanagan, or J.T. as his mom called him is here, weighing in at 7 pounds 8 ounces he is healthy and happy. They will let everyone see him soon."

The back-slapping and happy tears are so indicative of this group of people that I wonder how I ever considered leaving. This is my family, these crazy bikers, their woman and their children, what a boring life I'd have without them. And now, I have Paul too.

Once the baby has been taken care of and they are in their room, Everyone is allowed to go see Cat and Fox, look at J.T. and give their congratulations. Josie is on cloud nine, and Ranger is looking forward to retiring someday and building a motorcycle with J.T., but then Lissey overheard that bit of planning and decided it was time to set her grandpa straight on a few things.

"Grandpa, you are going to have to help me build a motorcycle first. I am the oldest, and I can't be a Road Warrior without a bike."

"I'll gladly help you build a motorcycle baby girl, but you know you can't be a patched Road Warrior Lissey, you are a girl," Ranger tells her.

"Yes, I can, you can change the rules grandpa." And the discussion continues with Lissey trying to explain to her grandfather that he needs to change the rules to allow girls to patch into the club, yes, this argument again.

Cat watches her daughter and father-in-law with quiet indulgence. Lissey is a fourth-generation princess, a Warrior Angel in her own right, the oldest of the Original's great-grandchildren. If anyone can get the old guard to change the rules, well it may be Lissey. BlackJack, one of the Originals, and Fox's grandfather, still to this day spends at least two days a week with Cat and Fox, telling Lissey all the stories of his time, the founding of the RWMC, and encouraging Lissey to take life by the horns and make her way in a blaze of glory. Lissey, if anyone, could turn this club around someday. But for now, the child was preparing for her fifth birthday and then starting kindergarten in the fall. Motorcycles and patches are a thing of the future for this little princess.

"You know Ranger, she starts school this fall." Cat reminds him.

"The fuck you say!" he looks startled.

"Yep, the princess is leaving the palace, six hours a day."

"Not sure I like that idea too much." Ranger is looking at Fox now. "Private school, Fox. With security. We need to find a couple of security types to prospect in. They can just be Lissey's bodyguards." Ranger continues. And damn but the man is serious.

"No, boys." Cat interrupts. "She can go to school like all the other little girls, play on the playground, run and fall, and even have crushes. She isn't going into a bubble."

"Ok Kitty Cat, no bubble. But, she will have security."

The men spent the next half hour discussing security, which is how the RWMC was setting up their own security company. Complete with a bevy of private detectives, security specialists, and even some bond enforcement agents. Another legal income stream for the MC, and guaranteed security for the growing population of the RWMC children.

Chapter Thirteen

Pipes:

With all the excitement of Fox and Cat's new baby, J.T., and the new patch-overs from other charters, it took nearly a week for me to get Trinity to Sinners and her brand done. She, Cat, and Rory had come up with an idea for the brand, but none of the girls are very artistic, so we took the idea to Sinner and let him draw up a design based on their idea. Once it was completed, we went to Sinner's shop to see the final drawing and get the brand started.

It was intricate and had a lot of detail, color, and shading so Sinner thought it would take at least two sittings, maybe three to complete. Since this was Rory's first tat, and she was not sure how she'd do with the pain, we agreed to take it slow and give her frequent breaks.

The design was a guitar, done in amber and black with the Property of Pipes done in the Barrel of the guitar. Coming out of the guitar are musical notes, and within the notes are the words Paul and Trinity and the date I patched her. She added some other frilly design accents to it and she decided to put it on her right shoulder on the back. I of course am ecstatic. To mark herself as mine, forever, and use my talent as part of the brand, well, it humbled me. This stunning creature is putting my name, my road name, my talent, and my love on her flawless body for the world to see – amazing!

Today, after letting it heal she is doing a reveal at the clubhouse, Pipe Dreams is playing tonight, and Trinity is wearing a beautiful white tube top with a pair of hip hugger short shorts, and sandals. Her hair is going up in a messy bun on top of her head and she is making sure her patch brand is showing. Her cut is staying off for a bit, so the brand is the focus. Later, as a lot of people start partying, to avoid any accidental deaths, of the jealous man type, she will have to put the cut back on over the tube top. But, for the earlier part of the evening, the brand alone will be enough.

Trinity:

I am nervous, Mom is going to the clubhouse tonight with dad and Joker to watch Pipes band. I am dressing a bit revealing, but I want to show off my brand. I showed mom and dad the ring Pipes bought me for our engagement and mom cried. I think she thought I'd be his Old Lady, but not a wife. I knew all along that once we decided to be together, we'd marry too. I love that man so much. I think the sweet butts have accepted that they have to keep hands off him, and me kicking out that club whore last week was a good method lesson for them all.

Party nights bring in the hangers-on though, the ones that only come for the parties and hookups. They may not realize that he is off-limits so, I will be there, front and center, ready to teach any lessons that need to be taught. Our Angel's Crew has come up with some rules, and we've decided our crew is going to be like the RWMC, we are a sisterhood, we will have each other's back and we'll be there for each other through everything. And, we'll watch out for each other where our men are concerned too. No bitches will poach! If an old lady or steady girlfriend is not around, and someone tries to poach – we kick ass!

"Hey girl, are you ready to go?" Raven is at my door. Since the band is meeting early, and Rory is with Snake, Raven and I are riding our bikes to the clubhouse together. Nice to have another woman that rides as I do. Raven is so much like me, I don't know why we were not better friends before now.

"Yeah, come on in. Need to grab a couple of things then we can hit it." I yell back to her.

"Wow, chickee, you're all packed up. Have you found a house yet?"

"No, but Pipes has a list for us to go look at tomorrow from the realtor."

"Good luck, grab your short shorts for tonight girl, I have mine too so we'll both be sluts". Raven says.

"Yeah, just wearing these leather pants and boots for the ride in. Looks hot with the tube top too though."

"Yep, where is your cut?"

"Here," I say, grabbing it up and putting it on for the ride into the club."

"Let's roll then. I told Fletch I'd be there early, he wants me to meet someone, he is trying to fix me up with some guy he met. The damn fool doesn't realize I don't like pussy's and those are the guys he always seems to find for me."

"It's his way of keeping control sweetie. If you get a badass, then he won't be able to control him and he wants to let you have a man – but not one he can't control."

"That is fucked up Trinity, how do you know that?"

"Have you met my brother yet?" I laugh at her, knowing full well she knows Joker.

"Guess that makes sense."

After we arrive at the club, Raven goes to meet up with her brother, and I go looking for my man.

"Hey there handsome, I'm looking for a man to fulfill all my wild girl fantasies. Do you know anyone like that?" I ask Pipes as he is tuning his guitar and setting up for the night.

"Well, it just so happens," He laughs, stepping off the stage and wrapping me in his arms. "I have just the man in mind."

"Hmm, well, I could ditch my boyfriend and take you home with me if you'd like to try," I tell him.

"Well, we could start by…" and he begins to whisper lots of wonderful ideas into my ear, as I laugh and in a couple of cases I actually blush.

"Trinity!" I hear Raven shout at me. I turn in Pipes' arms, towards my friend as she runs over to us, an angry stare in her eyes.

"You will NOT believe it. That idiot introduced me to a new prospect who is only eighteen years old!"

"You are kidding?" I gasp.

"No, I was polite, told the prospect I was too old for him, then told my brother to pound rocks!"

"Hang with me tonight. I'll introduce you to some people, your own age – or older."

"No pussy boys!" she insists. "Too bad you found Pipes first, that is one hot man you have Trinity," she adds, winking at Pipes.

"There are always my brothers Styx & Rayne, they are twins, and a lot like me, in lots of ways," he remarks, and winking makes Raven blush a pretty shade of pink.

I laugh and promise, real men only, then turn back to my man for some last-minute kisses before leaving to change into my short shorts and sandals. I am ready to show off the brand.

Mom is scandalized by my attire, dad laughs it off and tells her it's now Pipes problem. Joker just shakes his head but is impressed with the ink. Cat and Fox are here for a while, Josie is babysitting, and Ranger is here for a bit too, but Penny is causing him some problems now that she has joined Angel's Crew and is starting to show signs of being corrupted by the rest of us. Cat took me in the bathroom and showed me her ink and the tat she has of the forever Fox on her breast. Have to say, I like my brand better, but those forever tat's are cool. Penny informed me she is getting the angel wings done next week at Sinner's Ink but she isn't telling her folks or anyone but the Crew. We've all decided to come up with a tat design for the Crew, that we can all get done. We are working on it now. Someday all the old lady's and such will have it. Sinner thinks it is a good idea, so he'll keep our secret and help us.

I've only had one beer, wanting to keep my shit together for a while in case I have to hurt anyone messing with my man, but the band is getting ready to start so I am grabbing a beer and taking my seat with my folks and going to watch my man use that beautiful voice of his to seduce the masses.

Pipe's Dream

Raven joins us as the band is starting their first song. Pipes calls out to me and dedicates his first song to his beautiful old lady and soon to be wife, which makes me smile the whores boo, and mom and dad shake their heads.

He starts to sing an Ed Sheeran love song, Perfect, and I am swooning, knowing all that man is mine, when Raven starts pulling at me wanting to know who that sexy drummer is. Uh Oh, Styx has an admirer.

"That man is so sexy!" Raven tells me. "Where has he been all my life?"

"He is Pipes's brother, Rayne is his twin."

"Wow, that is one talented family," Raven says.

"With all those moves and muscles, he must be all man!" she says.

"He is a good man, but a bit moody too. Most musicians are." I say.

"I want to meet him, Trinity!"

"Ok, see what I can arrange," I tell her.

Then we decide to dance. Raven and I grab Penny and Rory and we go to the front and start to dance. Cat declines since she is still recovering from having J.T., but she gives us her blessing to shake our stuff. She still isn't drinking alcohol either since she is nursing, but she is happy to be out for the evening.

Rory and I have brands, and Rory has her cut on, so we are not bothered by men, but Penny, who is dressed hot as sin for a change has men trying to get her to dance constantly. Uncle Ranger is NOT happy and twice Fox had to cut in to keep Ranger from cutting in. That would have been the end of Penny's hopes of any man dancing with her.

Raven is an absolute loony bin tonight. She is dancing, drinking, and laughing. Men are drawn to her like moths to a flame. She just bursts with happiness. Her worry about meeting men was for nothing. Every red-blooded man in the club that is unattached and unrelated is watching her and wanting her. She has two men dancing with her at once, one in front, one in back. If she goes home alone tonight I will be surprised.

I notice Styx is watching her too, Hmm, that could be interesting.

Pipes has his share of groupies, yelling out requests and one bitch was stupid enough to flash her tits at him. I of course had a pleasant talk with her, one that caused her to blanch white as a ghost and decide to make an early night of it.

Pipes saw and laughed when he saw the woman leave.

After their set was over, Pipes and I decided to call it a night and went home to get some sleep since we have house hunting to do tomorrow morning.

Pipes:

Looking at houses with Trinity is a job. To say she is picky about homes would be an understatement. She is determined that the home we purchase will be our forever home. I tried to tell her in a few years we may want to move up a bit, but nope, she says she will be here for a long time, and eventually, it will go to our children.

So, finally, we are going to house number five of the day. This is one that I hope she likes. It is my favorite. It is in the little unincorporated Blue Diamond area, where the lots are all over an acre, some as large as five acres. The one we are going to now is on two acres, has a sprawling ranch style adobe home on it with a concrete wall surrounding the entire home and an iron access gate. I like the ability to secure the property. She will like the pool and casita that are out in the back by the pool.

Trinity is in love with it. She has already decided how to decorate, wants to set the casita up as a studio for me and the band to play in, and has decided that she is going to get a huge dog or two since she is no longer in an apartment and no one can tell her she can't have pets. Of course, I tell her to go for it, she can have anything she wants now that she agreed to be my wife.

The selling point for me is the four-car garage, her car, my car, the SUV we'll need for when kids come along, and room for our bikes. Perfect.

The realtor has assured us we can close within two weeks, so we are going to measure rooms and go shopping for furniture later today. We found a house! Thank fuck!

Chapter Fourteen

(Moving day: three weeks later)

Trinity:

Oh my god is it ever going to be over? I am so tired, cranky, and hungry. I want food, sleep, and sex! I am tired of living out of boxes, It seems like I can never get enough sex, I am always hungry and I am tired constantly.

"Paul! Where is the box with my spices? Damn, I need to make some food before we leave with the kitchen stuff."

"Baby, your mom is on her way and she is bringing food, no more cooking. The Prospects will be here soon and moving all the boxes."

"Ok, good, I am starving."

"Why don't you eat, then you and your mom go on over to the new house and wait for us to bring stuff. All you need to do is get the bedroom set up tonight, then we'll work on the rest tomorrow."

"Ok, I am not working for a week, so I can get stuff done."

"I am ok tonight and tomorrow but then we have gigs all the rest of the week." Pipes says.

"I know hot stuff, I'm going to come to Rage on Wednesday. No girls night for you if I am off. Anyway, the Crew is having ladies night we are introducing Raven to Rage and our girls time." I tell him.

"Glad I'm going to be there for that!" he says.

"Me too."

"I'd better not see anyone messing with you!" he tells me.

"I love you, we can watch out for each other," I tell him.

The next morning:

The first night in our new home was anticlimactic. After all the excitement, the moving, our new furniture being delivered, and the family bringing food for us and the help unpacking. Well, we were so exhausted that we fell into bed without much more than a brief kiss goodnight.

I haven't hung the curtains in our room yet, so the first beam of morning light that reached my side of the bed woke me. Stretching I looked to see Pipes still sound asleep next to me, his face covered by one arm, most likely to keep out the light. Fortunately for me, he was sleeping on his back because I've decided to wake him up with a surprise.

After a quick trip to the bathroom, I slip back into bed and pull the covers over my head. Then I work my way down to the bottom of the mattress to where I find the object of my desire. Listening to ensure he is still sleeping, I hear the steady breathing that convinces me my mission is still a go.

I snuggle myself between his legs and using my head to hold up the covers enough to see what I am getting into, I flick out my tongue and give the tip of his cock a light lick, taking special care to play around with that sexy as shit piercing he has. I watch

141

as it starts to grow under my attention and even bobs a bit in my direction as though he has a mind of his own and is saying good morning to me, despite Pipes still being asleep.

I decide to reward the greeting with a long slow lick along the underside of the entire, long beautiful sword that has become one of my favorite parts of Pipes's body. I am rewarded with even more growth and as the inches spread out to his full length, I start to take it into my mouth fully, working him in and out of my mouth, tasting the precum that alerts me to the fact that Pipes breathing has changed, and now I feel his hands slide down under the covers and grip my hair.

Knowing he is awake now, I begin to get excited myself, I want to give him the best wake up I can, knowing that he will soon reciprocate, and I will be screaming in ecstasy myself as well.

I feel him responding more and more as he starts to use my hair to push and pull my head up and down his cock, setting the rhythm for me, I am taking him so deep into my mouth that he is pushing into my throat, so I start swallowing, to prevent my gag reflex, which causes him to groan and to push even harder.

"Oh god, baby, fuck! That feels so good."

I can't say anything to him, my face being so full of his enormous cock, but I take my hands an I reach down and stroke him from the base, down to his balls. I massage his balls and feel them draw uptight, I know he is getting close.

"Oh, baby, I'm close, hmm, I'm going to cum, soon baby, I'm ahh, god!"

Pipe's Dream

And then he explodes in my mouth, and god he tastes so good, so I take all of him, every drop, every bit, and lick him clean like I'm licking a lollipop. Until he is pulling me by my hair, up next to him where he is kissing me and slipping my sleep shirt off my body in one fluid motion.

"Good Morning baby," I say to him.

"Fuck yeah, that was an amazing wake-up Trinity." And then my man pulls me up, onto his chest so that I am straddling him. He reaches up and plays with the nipple rings on my breasts for a minute while he is kissing my belly, then reaching for my ass, he pulls me up and onto his face.

"My turn now baby, I want to taste that hot sweet pussy."

And taste me he does, I am so turned on from the time I spent on him, that it only takes a minute for me to get off on his face, and chuckling at my quick response, he pulls me back down and sits me on his lap, again straddling him, but this time, lifting me, he sets me down on his erection.

Our laughing and smiles disappear quickly as the intense pleasure of our joining overtake all other emotions, and I feel the rush of desire overtaking my whole body.

"Oh baby, that feels so damn good." I moan into his chest, as I lean down and kiss him on first one nipple and then the other. I love rubbing my face in the slight scattering of chest hair he has. It is intoxicating.

Even though he just had a hard orgasm, Pipes is raring to go and begins to fuck me so sweetly that I want to cry with pleasure at the love I feel from this soft seduction. Seeing my mood, Pipes decides it is time to change things up.

143

Raven Featherwood

Putting his arms through my legs and grasping my knees, he rolls us over so that I am not on the bottom and he is pulling my legs up and over his shoulders. Gripping me by the knees he opens me up so that he can look down and watch as his trusting in and out of me, harder and deeper than before.

"Oh baby, I love to watch my cock fuck your pussy, damn sexy sight." He pants, as the sweat drips from his body onto mine.
Pushing up on my elbows, I look between us, at the sight that is so mesmerizing to Pipes, and yeah, it is fucking amazing the way we fit together.

"Fuck baby, I can't believe you fit inside me as big as you are," I gasp out, falling back down as his trusts begin to get harder, pushing me up to the headboard.

"I. Fuck. I love you, Trinity!"

"Paul, baby, I'm close, don't stop, please."

"Please what baby? Tell me."

"Please, ah, don't stop fucking me."

"Ok, I'm not, take me, babe, take all of me."

And then he gives me all of him. The pounding he gives me is one I know I will still feel days from now, I am pushed too tight into the headboard that I can no longer move, but still, he pounds into me, hard, deep strokes. Pulling almost completely out of me, then pushing back into me in one long hard stroke, he grinds his hips with each complete stroke until I am screaming and panting out his name.

144

"That's it, scream for me baby, scream my name!"

And I do, as my entire body reacts to his fucking and I start to tremble, out of control while my entire body convulses on his cock, milking him dry as he cums with me and we know that there is no way the entire neighborhood has not heard the wake-up call.

Good Morning.

Chapter Fifteen

Pipes:

Monday morning, I am heading to the clubhouse for church, our Monday morning ritual. Trinity was still sleeping when I left, kissing that beautiful mouth gently I laid a rose on the pillow next to her and a note telling her I'd be home soon.

Today we are going for a ride, taking the bikes and just riding for a bit. She needs to settle a bit, that girl of mine has been strung tight as a drum for the past week or two. I am not sure what is going on, but we need to relax, this move has been tough.

Friday night, instead of going to the club, we are jamming at home, I've told the guys we could have some other people over too, barbeque in the back, play some music, swim, and party a bit. It will be our first party at the new house.

I am so excited to show off the casita to the guys. The bedroom is no more, we opened that room up to the living area, and now we've put chairs, small couches, and lots of lounging areas, and set it up for jamming and practicing. I've hung all kinds of music memorabilia on the walls, and Trinity even took my three older guitars that I don't use anymore and had them mounted and did a wall design with them as the feature. Totally cool looking.

The kitchen is stocked and set up for jam sessions too. A wine and beer cooler, beer on tap, popcorn machine, hot dog rollers, and the fridge is all junk food and fun food. My girl is so cool.

We are meeting Friday at noon to jam, and then the company is invited to come over at four, and we will barbeque and party all evening. We ordered a wet bar for the pool area, complete with a cabana-style bar set up, and Trinity said that she is going to do mixed drinks and have Scooter, a prospect that sometimes helps out at Rage serve drinks on Friday. I am looking forward to it.

Walking into church, I toss my cell into the tub of phones, and I go with Joker to the far side of the room to ask if he is coming Friday, and to suggest inviting a few girls to round things off for single men, have them come after seven so dinner is over. I know the boys, some of the brothers, and such would appreciate the women.

"Ok brothers, listen up," Ranger says.

"I want to go over the business stuff first. We've decided and now implemented another business. This provides another opportunity for those of you that are looking for more income to join up. Also, our Treasurer indicates the ROI on this business is one year only, so our overall income should see a boost in a second year."

"Fabulous Prez, what is it?" Rayne asks.

"Dude, you got no time for another job Rayne, Styx says to him."

"Maybe not, but I can spend more money." He remarks to a room full of laughter.

"We've decided to start a security company. We will do security systems, bodyguards, protection, and we are going to be doing bounty hunting." Ranger says.

"Damn, I want in on that, Storm says."

"You got it Storm I'd like to meet with you, Fletch, Joker, and King after church to talk a bit more about this business.

"Geek, you will need to stay for that also," Ranger adds.

"All officers, our pay remains the same until next budget approval in September of next year. We sit nicely at one mil per year each. First Generation non-officers and all of the honor guards still sit at $500k per year and Second Generation at $350k and Fourth Generation will start at $250k per year, without added duties. Fourth Generation kids are too young to receive income at this time, so their money is voided to the general fund, which is paying for their schools and security details for them or the women. Prospects are making $40k per year, and new patches without generational status are making $100k per year before any salary from the businesses." Ranger rattles this off as if no one knows, but with so many newly patched over members, it is a good time to reiterate the salary structure.

"Now, we are up to about twenty-five legit businesses everyone. They are all profitable especially the casino and cat house in Pahrump. Our interest in Rage is very profitable and Snake man you are doing a great job there. The strippers are producing a lot of income, and downstairs has picked up to the point we are up forty percent this year. Pin Stripes just sponsored a little league and a triple-A baseball team. We will generate income from baseball, and the alley itself is doing great with sixteen different leagues using the facility." He continues and off and on giving praises as he can and making sure everyone knows which businesses are ours and which are being purchased.

"The other thing I want to discuss is the new mall being put in out in the South Point area. We own about thirty acres in that area. We'd like to consider putting in a family compound there for people that need to purchase homes. We are getting more and more families, and I see the potential for having more kids and families than our current clubhouse can handle during a lockdown. We can build a fully gated and walled safe compound. The walls can be tall, electric on top with state of the art security. We can build fifty houses, each on a half-acre, with a pool and play area. Each house can have a safe room with an escape route. The remaining five acres can be for streets, a clubhouse, and a community park. The cost is high, but we can resell the homes to members only. It could take some of the stress off the clubhouse during lockdowns because the neighborhood would be equally safe. Our security company would handle all security for the community. What do you think? The land is paid for and we have a construction company so building costs will be going right back into another of our bank accounts. Out of budget will be some things like attorney costs, and fees for permits that sort of stuff. We will do all phases through Warrior Construction."

The idea got a unanimous vote in favor and many of the men present were interested in purchasing in the community, already dubbed Warrior Ranch Homes. I think that I should buy one of the homes myself, that way someday, Trinity and I will have a safe home for our children if we need it.

Trinity:

"Raven don't forget, Wednesday night is Ladies Night, the Crew is going out for it and we should have our patches by then too. So, we can all wear our cuts."

"I am so excited Trinity, I feel like I finally belong somewhere. I love the patch design too, it is pretty amazing." Raven says.

We decided on a skull, with wings that are surrounded by flowers. It looks nice and it has Warrior Angel's Crew for a top rocker, then if someone is Property, on the bottom they can add their Property of whomever, so they can wear it out on Lady's Night without losing the protection of the property patch. Anyone not attached doesn't have a bottom rocker. We are all excited about our cuts. Angel's crew has become quite the talk around the club too. The guys have started calling us the pussy patrol since we also go after vengeance for our own.

"I showed it to my Uncle Ranger before getting the cuts ordered," I told her.

"What did he say?"

"He thought it was a good idea. Said it lets us stand out as a group when we go out. Also, easier for the men to keep an eye on us when we are out together."

149

"It does make sense." She said.

"So, we'll pick you up or want to meet at the club?"

"Let's all meet at the clubhouse so we can put on our cuts before leaving."

"See you then"

Pipes:

I can't stay focused tonight, Snake is struggling too. The women are having ladies night tonight and they had these Crew cuts made for their pussy patrol. They were dressing and putting them on tonight at the club before coming to Rage. I wish I could have been there to see them. All the club was getting a reveal, but I had to be here to set up. Damn.

I keep watching the door for them. They are coming in a club SUV so they can either go home in the SUV without worrying about drinking or they can go with their men. I plan to put my woman on my bike tonight.

Chasity, one of the barmaids brought us all drinks and tried to get a bit friendly. I see why Trinity worries about the women. Until I started to pay attention to it, I never really noticed how often women touch me. Even casual touches, things I'd never have noticed before. I do now, because I know if a man casually touched my woman I'd chop his fucking hand off. She is right, I need to respect her claim on my body if I plan to push my claim on hers. And I damn well do plan to!

150

Pipe's Dream

We are getting close to starting time and I'd hoped they would be here in time, I like singing my first song to her. And then the noise level goes up a bit and Caro, my sister jumps up and runs off stage, she is bouncing like fucking Tigger as she runs up to the girls. And damn, they do look sexy. All of them have on black leather skirts, white tank tops, and sexy as all black heeled boots, then those cuts! Black and white, leather, and their patches. Trinity comes right up to the front, pulls her hair up into a messy bun and clips it, then turns around to show me the patch, and on the bottom, Property of Pipes is on the bottom rocker.

"Baby!" she shouts up to me, "I'm not going out, even with the ladies, without showing that I am your woman baby." Damn, she makes me hot.

"I love you girl!" I shout back to her.

And then it is time to get started. I look around and my sister has one of Angel's Crew cuts on too, damn that's cute.
"Are you ladies ready to party?" I shout out. And of course, the place goes ape shit. Lady's Night is vicious.

"We are starting our first set out tonight, as requested, as a tribute to Journey. And, as is fast becoming a custom for me, when my woman is present, this first song is for you baby."

Trinity jumps up and shouts I love you to me, then we start in with *When you Love a Woman*, and six other Journey hits follow before we take a break. The second half of the set is requests, women can fill out request forms and we pick six or seven during the break to sing. I spotted my girls' handwriting immediately, hers also had P&T in a heart on the upper corner, a dead giveaway. So, I started with her request, Marc Anthony's *You sang to Me*.

151

When we were nearing the end of our set, Trinity and the girls, who'd been dancing all through the set went to the VIP section to have a drink and rest, when I noticed a few bold men going up to the area to try to talk to the women. Raven was receptive and was talking like she was happy to have the attention, but one of the men took Trinity's hand like he was trying to pull her over to talk, She pulled away and I saw her shaking her head no, then she pointed to me and told the guy something. He looked at me and I stopped playing, I stopped mid-song and told the man to back off. What the fuck? I heard laughter from beside and behind me. Rayne grabbed the microphone in front of him and laughingly told the crowd we'd be taking one more request since Pipes was sidetracked by some douche trying to hit on his woman. Good save.

The women had fun, and no one was shit faced, but afterward, I noticed that Raven and Styx were standing together talking, and it looked serious, hm, I wonder about that, but then she goes off to the SUV and Styx goes to the bar, so must not have been anything.

I grab my girl and reminding everyone about the barbeque Friday night, then we take off for home, and some love play of my own.

Chapter Sixteen

Trinity:

"Babe, how many people did we invite to this party?" I ask Pipes when at about nine at night, five SUVs from the clubhouse show up full of people.

"A few, why?"

"We just had about thirty more show up, and sweet butts and club women with them," I say to him.

"I didn't think it would matter about the girl's Trinity, all the men don't have women, a party is more fun with someone to dance with." He says to me. And I have to admit, it's true.

"All the Crew woman have our cuts on, and I notice the hookups that are happening, including Raven and Styx," I tell him.

"Yeah, I noticed them talking Wednesday night too, is there something going on that I should know about?" he asks me.

"I know she thinks he's hot, but nothing else."

"Interesting."

So all night I am watching my girl crew keeping a watch to see what is going on. I see Caro isn't having too good a time and I go sit by her to see what is going on.

"Caro, hey girl, why the long face?"
"Just dealing, that's all." She says.

"Who is he girl?"

"I'd rather not say, don't want to make an ass of myself."

"What, like I did for years with Pipes?" I say to her.

"Well, actually, Pipes and you were friends at one point, and he did love you. The object of my unrequited affection doesn't even know I exist."

"Tell me little sister, who is it?"

"You won't say anything? To anyone?" she is serious, and since she is Pipes's baby sister, it's time I step up the loyalty to her.

"Nope, sister power girl, we keep each other's secrets."

"Joker." She tells me.

"Wow, you aim high, don't you? You know my brother is a man whore, right?"

"That was what everyone said about Pipes too."

"True."

"He kissed me once." She tells me.

Pipe's Dream

"When?" I ask, surprised.

"Last month at the big party when the new patch members
were here." He was dancing with me, we were in a dark part of the
club, and he told me I was beautiful, a rose not quite opened yet,
and he kissed me. I haven't been able to forget that kiss."
"Well damn. He is watching Caro, if you are serious about
him then we need to step up the game, you need to show some
maturity, soon."

"How?"

"Pipe Dreams, are they playing next week at Rage?"

"Tuesday, Wednesday, and Thursday." She says. Then the
club on the weekend.

"Ok, tell the guys you want to lead Tuesday and you are
singing three PINK songs. For your set."

"I love singing PINK, I am good with her songs. But they
are pretty mellow, at least the ones I've sung in the past."

"This week you won't be singing those. Her album *The
Truth About Love* has a couple that will shake him up, AND, you
need to dress the part. I'll help you. In the meantime, I'll send you
a list of songs you need to practice."

"Thank you, but how will we get him there?"
"Leave that to me. He'll be there."

And so, I plan to help my girl out – with my brother.

155

Raven Featherwood

Epilogue

Pipes:

My life is finally something that I can look at with pride, fulfillment, and hope. I can't believe it, I have this amazing woman that loves me. An extended family that I am proud to have in my life. My brothers, the MC, the band. I just don't know how my life could become any fuller.

Trinity has decided to stop bartending. She is going to keep the books at the new security company. Her brother asked her if she'd become their Bookkeeper and help with scheduling, she loves it because it is daytime hours, giving her the evenings off to come out when I play. She still doesn't like it when I am on a gig without her, she trusts me as I trust her. But, women like band members. Combine that with the biker persona and I get my share of offers, but not when Trinity is around. Word has spread about the Angel Crew, or as we brothers lovingly call them the pussy patrol. These gals don't take any shit! Just last week a hanger-on tried to hit on Fox when he was at the club. Cat was home with the kids and he was only out for a few drinks with us. A club whore sat on his lap and tried to proposition him. Trinity, Rory, Raven, and Caro snatched that bitch up by the hair and gave her an ass-kicking she won't likely forget. They called Cat and told her about it too. Fifteen minutes later, Cat, with a sleepy Lissey and baby J.T. showed up. She proceeded o hand the baby to Fox, put Lissey in Joker's arms, and went to the bitch and proceeded to kick her ass again. Nope, the bitches need to back the fuck off or they won't like the outcome.

Fox, by the way was tickled pink. Told his "kitty cat" that she was so sexy when she kicked ass that he needed to take her home and fuck her brains out. She just smiled and told him she'd be waiting and not to be too long. He followed her out.

Yeah, I am one blessed man.

I need to get dressed for the gig tonight at Rage. Trinity said she bought the band new shirts to wear tonight, she told us to wear whatever to the gig, and she'd provide our new shirts before we went on stage.

"Caro, girl, do you know anything about these shirts Trinity wants us to wear tonight?" I ask my sister.

"Yes, as a matter of fact, I saw them." She tells me.

"Well, how about a clue?"

"Nope, girl power brother, we stick together." She tells me.

"Boys and girls," Trinity calls out from the dance floor. "I have something for you all."

I notice she has her cut on and it is zipped completely up so you can't even see her tee. Hm, must be part of the surprise.

"Ok baby, what are these shirts we are wearing?" I ask her.

"Well, baby, I'd like you to wear these shirts tonight, just for me, ok?"

"Ok, but can we see them?" I am exasperated. Then I notice that Snake is watching, with a shit-eating grin on his face. He knows the fucker!

I take the shirt from my woman and opening it I see a picture of one of those stick tests, for pregnancy, that says positive on it. Above the picture is the wording, Daddy to Be. The bandmember's shirts all say Uncle to Be.

Ok, so it could get better!

The End

(Well, for now anyway......)

Trinity and Pipe's story isn't over yet, stay tuned for *Happily Ever After*. Trinity and Pipes will finally tie the knot, biker style. Along with a lot of crazy shenanigans by the RWMC, the Warrior Angels will have a few surprises up their sleeves, showing that once and for all the fairer sex is by no means the weaker sex....

159

Raven Featherwood

About the Author

Life has a wonderful way of throwing you curve balls. Some are more traumatic than others, but all of them help to make you the person that you are this very day. My personal curveball was starting over again, in my 50's after being married most of my life and raising seven children.

As with any of life's challenges, you make of it what you will, and I decided to once again, pick up the pen (or keyboard) and begin to write. It never ceases to amaze me how just giving free rein to these musings has allowed me to begin to heal my own heart, spirit, and mind.

My life is simple; while having a blast writing this series of books, I spend a lot of time hiking and fishing in the many parks, forests, and lakes surrounding my new home in Fort Smith Arkansas. I was given a second chance at love with an amazing man that daily shows me that life in my golden years can be as exciting as it was at twenty. I am also blessed to live near several of my children and grandchildren which makes daily life exhilarating.

I often tell my friends and family that I don't have multiple personalities, but I do have many interesting characters running around in my mind trying to break free and share their stories. I've decided to allow them to escape the confines of that limited space, and in doing so, share with you all their lives, loves, and ultimately their Happily Ever After.

Books in the Series

I hope you enjoy the lives of the members of the Road Warrior's Motorcycle Club. As they share with me their unique life stories, I will continue to share them with you.

Welcome to the world of the Road Warrior's Motorcycle Club. Based in the Las Vegas Valley, the Road Warrior's MC was formed by five former Vietnam Vets looking for a sense of family, that brotherhood they left behind when they left the military. This is the story of their club, now, three generations later, their children and grandchildren are taking up the torch as the RWMC goes into the future. These are their stories, their lives, their hopes, dreams, challenges, and their HEA's.

BOOK ONE
Forever My Own

FOX:
The minute I met CATRIONA I was lost. Her beauty and innocence called to me like a siren. There was a place inside of me that I didn't know existed, a place just waiting to be filled with her light, her caring, her heart. But, with one miscommunication, one failed connection, I lost it all, hell I lost more than I even realized. Until four years later when my entire world came crashing down on me, in the form of a precocious three-year-old pixie named Felicity.

I will get my family back, I will earn the trust of the only woman to ever touch my heart. But, as quickly as I start to see a possible happily ever after for my little family, it is all gone, she is gone. See, I am a member of the Road Warrior's MC and our enemies have my woman, and they are not known for their care of the fairer sex. Somehow, I must find her, then, find a way to help her, because being lost in that mess is sure to leave her broken.

CAT:
He was my first, my only, but he abandoned me and our child. It has taken me years, but I am better, happy even. But now he's returning home, and I have to find peace with him. But what about our daughter, will he man up and acknowledge his daughter? After abandoning me in my pregnancy, I don't know what to expect.

Then, as if my troubled past wasn't filled with enough heartache, I am dragged into a war, not of my making and my life will never be the same again. How do you survive something like this? Will I ever be able to see my child and Fox again? After what I have become, not likely. How do you survive something like this? And even then, how do you ever look that precious innocent child in the face after becoming what I've become?

BOOK TWO
Snake's Rage

Snake:
My mind is blown! All I needed was some damn help in the bar. Not more trouble in the form of a leggy sex kitten that made me lose my damn mind. If only Cat wasn't still so fragile, I wouldn't be needing another bartender. One minute I was wishing I had some help and the next this hot as hell redhead is dirty dancing on my bar with me. Of course, I hired her. That sinfully delicious body, and those innocent eyes.

Talk about standing at attention, every nerve in my body was aware of her. It may have been a bit over the top, what happened in my office while supposedly doing her new hire paperwork. But I couldn't resist the pull. She possessed me as much as I possessed that tight body of hers. I need more of that, at least a little more, enough to get her out of my system. I will never let a woman get to me, get inside my head, ever again. Besides, being a Road Warrior, I have all the women I want, I will never again let feelings for a woman dictate my actions. Not going there, no matter how hot she is or how my body aches for her.

Rory:

I got the job! Let's hope I keep it. Sleeping with the boss is never a good idea. But he is so hot and talk about put together. He has the most magnificent body; it just makes me ache to run my hands all over him. I can't believe it, a new job, and a hot man. Next, I'll get an apartment, and see where this new relationship takes me. I hope back into his arms, I just need to touch him, kiss him, taste him.

Yes, it's time to move on, let the past go, live in the now. Too bad my past doesn't agree with my new outlook, and in fact, it is about to intrude on my idyllic fantasy. See, my past, my rapists, are Road Warriors too.

His brothers and his club? Or the woman who is fast becoming the very reason his heartbeats? As their pasts collide with their futures, will Rory and Snake be able to overcome and be together or will the pull of the past finally win out?

Coming Soon

BOOK FOUR
Styx Beat

Pipe's brother Styx has met his match in the seductive Raven. His world is about to take a drastic change – no matter how hard he fights it.

BOOK FIVE
Joker's Fantasy

Joker has always thought Caro was the most beautiful woman/child he'd ever seen. But the age gap, and her overprotective brothers, keep him at arm's length. But then even the best-laid plans….

BOOK SIX
King's Folly

King is too much the macho man to ever fall for a pretty face. And with his new responsibilities at Ace of Spades Investigations, he certainly doesn't need the pretty distraction that comes in the form of the pretty new barmaid, Arianna.

But Ari has a secret, she isn't who she claims to be.

THE PREQUEL

The Road Warrior's